Werewolves 101

By Marisa Claire

Contents:

CHAPTER ONE

"So, which house are you hoping to get in?"

I dropped a pair of jeans back into my half-unpacked suitcase and turned toward the chipper voice of my new roommate, who kept blabbering on about the pros and cons of her two picks without even waiting for my reply. She sat on the edge of her twin bed across the room—AKA six feet away—swinging her feet a good three inches above the gray tiled floor. Her blue-streaked black hair stood out sharply against the white cinder block wall, and her wide brown eyes were practically swirling with magic.

In other words, she was exactly the sort of person I had been trying to get *away* from when I chose the solid, no-nonsense Keller Parks State College for my alma mater. And yet here she was...

I had already forgotten her name. It had been right there next to mine in glittering, construction paper letters on the outside of the heavy wooden door we'd be sharing until sometime next May. And she'd introduced herself just twenty minutes earlier when I'd slunk through that door after her overly doting parents finally went away. But social graces had never really been my thing, even under the best of circumstances—which these were clearly not.

I glanced down at her shirt like maybe she'd be wearing a name tag to help me out. Instead, I came face-to-face with a screen print of those dudes from that demon hunter TV show that every single girl I'd ever had to live with loved, but which I totally didn't get. And, I mean, it's not like I never *tried* to see the appeal, to fit in with my ever-revolving cast of "sisters", but since none of their parents ever wanted to keep me around for an entire television season...

An irritated sigh escaped me. "Listen, uh...Nikki—?"

Please be her name.

"Um, actually, it's Hickoree." She extended her arms like branches above her head with an animated sway. "Like the tree. But with two e's... like a tree."

"Of course it is." I blew a breath out through my lips. "Listen, Hickoree, we'd better get this out of the way right now before you start unpacking your wand collection, expecting me to be impressed."

She glanced at the cardboard box to her left.

Ha, called it.

I held up my hands as if I could push all that geek energy away. "I'm not into that stuff. Like, however into it you are? That's how *not* into it I am. So, if we're going to be sharing this cell for the next nine months, let's make a pact right now that you keep all your funky-pop dragons or whatever on that side of the room..."

She glanced at the cardboard box to her right and pinched her lips together.

Ha, called it again.

I thrust my right hand out to her. "... and I won't throw any of them out the window. Deal?"

Hickoree slammed her hands to the boxes. I could pretty much hear the voice in her head wondering whether or not this threat was grounds to request a new roommate. Probably because the voice in mine had already been there, considered that. But Hickoree would've filled out the same Campus Housing Compatibility Form I did, the one with plenty of room to list our deal breakers on the last page, and I was certain that where I'd written "*no wannabe witches*" she'd written "*no normal people like Remi St. James.*"

Someone had done this to us on purpose.

Finally, Hickoree must've come to the same conclusion, because she grasped my hand for the briefest of handshakes, as though my allergy to whimsy might be contagious.

"Deal," she said. "But just so you know, the sorting ceremony is kind of, well, mandatory." She bit her glossy lower lip and winced like she thought I might slap her.

I tilted my head. "I beg your pardon?"

Hickoree handed me a bright orange piece of paper from the desk between our beds. It was the itinerary for Welcome Week, and, sure enough, scheduled for tonight in bold black letters:

SORTING CEREMONY 7 PM (MANDATORY).

"What the *actual* hell?" I exploded, staring at the words. "This is outrageous! This has to be some sort of infringement of my rights!"

Hickoree raised an eyebrow. "And what rights would those be, exactly?"

A whoosh of dizziness slammed into my brain. I raked a hand through my brown waves and felt beads of sweat forming on my forehead. Even *I* knew that was an extreme overreaction to the dorm's silly freshmen icebreaker party, but still, I couldn't seem to get a grip. The orange paper rattled in my trembling hands.

"Trust me," I choked out. "This is a direct violation of my liberty *and* pursuit of happiness."

"Well, two out of three ain't bad. At least your life isn't in danger," Hickoree offered, and now I did want to slap her because it wasn't fair that she was sitting there cool as a cucumber while I—the *normal* person—forgot how breathing worked.

I slapped the paper down on the desk instead and sank onto my bare mattress next to the single suitcase holding all my belongings. "How much time do I have to find a different college where this sort of thing doesn't happen?"

Hickoree reached for her phone, but it appeared to be lost somewhere inside the fortress of cardboard boxes on top of her bed. My stomach turned. Nobody brings their entire childhood bedroom to college, which meant this girl still had *more* magical knick-knacks at home. Just like all those fangirl foster "sisters" I'd lived with over the years, each one more determined than the last to be the homewrecker in my committed relationship with reality.

"Thirty minutes," Hickoree said, finally holding her phone up.

"That's not enough time, is it?"

She shook her head. "Probably not."

"Okay. Fine. I can do this." I slapped my hands on my knees. "But first, I'm going to take a walk. Yes. That's what I'll do."

But when I stood, all of my blood rushed into my head—or maybe away from my head, it was honestly impossible to tell. I just knew it was rushing, like it had some very important place to be with or without me. What I didn't know was that my knees were buckling, at least not until Hickoree's hand shot out and steadied me.

"I'm okay," I blurted before she could ask. "I'm fine. Really."

"Is it your blood sugar?" Hickoree asked, and then nodded like that explained everything. "I've been having trouble with low blood sugar lately. My pediatrician says I'm fine, just pre-college jitters, but it's like, I'm not a kid anymore, what does he know? So I think I'll go to—"

"I just need some air," I cut her off. "This room is so small. Isn't it small? And hot. Wow."

Her big brown eyes bounced around the walls of what was actually a fairly decent-sized room, finally landing on me, full of pity. "Well, it *is* the third floor. They do say heat rises."

I tugged at the collar of my shirt. "They do say that. Okay. I'm gonna go."

Her forehead wrinkled. "Do you want me to come with?"

I shook my head and waved her off me. "Nope. You stay right here. I bet you've got like a whole cosplay thing to put on for this."

"No, I was thinking for this I'd just wear the scarf. Maybe tip the scales in the right direction, but not totally embarrass myself if I get the wrong—" She clamped her lips together and mumbled, "Sorry."

"S'ok," I mumbled back, willing my legs not to stagger as I made my way to the door, trying not to think about the trail of striped scarves I'd left in donation boxes around Alabama. Gifts from all those foster "sisters" who'd lost my number the second their parents shipped me on to the next house.

I turned back with my hand on the knob. "You know it's still like ninety degrees out?"

She cocked her head. I waved my own question out of the air.

"Wait," she said, wiggling her phone at me. "Should we exchange numbers, just in case...?"

"Just in case what?" I laughed. "Oh no... you're one of those girls who forgets your keys, aren't you?"

She smiled and kind of rolled her eyes. "You sure do know me already."

I started out the door.

"Remi, seriously. If we're going to be roommates, I think we should exchange numbers."

With a sigh, I turned around and rattled off my number, then dutifully plugged hers into my phone.

"Thank you," she called as I swung out the door.

I popped my throbbing head back into the room. "Hey, Hickoree? If you do lose your keys, how about you just call it back with one of your wands?"

***

I could have been nicer. I *should* have been nicer. I knew that. Hickoree seemed like a perfectly likable person. Just because we had wildly different tastes in pop culture, that didn't give me license to treat her like crap. I'd need to apologize when I got back. Start fresh. Same ground rules, but... fresh.

My head felt better already as I wandered the campus with nice long strides and big deep breaths. I would need to explain to Hickoree about my anxiety attacks. The last thing I needed was her thinking I was some sort of basket case who had actually reacted that poorly to a silly sorting ceremony, which I knew was just an elaborate trick to get everyone in the dorm to pitch in with chores for the sake of earning points that would ultimately add up to nothing more than a year-end pizza party from some third-rate local chain.

No, the dizziness, the weakness—the rushiness?— that had been going on for months. It started sometime between my birthday and graduation. Mrs. Baker, the guidance counselor, told me I was just stressing too much about college; I'd do just fine in life wherever I ended up going. But I knew that already. The cool thing about being a relentlessly practical person is that you don't give yourself over to any pie-in-the-sky fantasies—not the wizards and dragons kind, nor the rich and famous in real life kind. All I had to do was go to college—*any* college— get a sensible degree like nursing or accounting, snag a job that paid well enough so I could buy a house— nothing fancy—and never have to move again for as long as I lived.

Reasonable, *achievable* dreams. That was my philosophy.

So why do I feel like I'm about to die half the time?

Up ahead, a cluster of future frat jerks were cat-calling girls from the steps of their dorm, so I cut across the grassy lawn toward the student center where I'd bought my books—about real things like Health and Public Speaking—earlier that day. Sweat trickled down my neck, but the normal kind that comes with August in Alabama, not the freaking out over nothing kind. A clock tower loomed over the courtyard, and in the same moment that I noticed it, the heavy bells inside began to chime.

Seven o'clock. Party time.

My phone buzzed, and I nearly jumped out of my skin. It never buzzed.

Pulling it out of my back pocket, I took one glance at the screen and my eyes nearly rolled out of my head.

Where are you?

My first text from Hickoree. But at least she'd spelled all the words out.

Ten points to whatever house she's hoping for.

I looked back in the direction of the dorm, then

ahead of me, past the clock tower, to a shadowy area in the distance between two brick buildings. Somehow I knew that was where I needed to be.

My phone buzzed again.

Please come back.

Seriously? I've been gone what? Fifteen minutes? She can't miss me that much.

I chewed on my lip and glanced at the dark space between the two buildings again. I absolutely did *not* need to be in the shadows between two buildings on the far side of campus. That was the opposite of sane, the one thing I had always prided myself on being.

Until recently.

My phone buzzed yet again, and I glanced down at a wall of text.

I don't want to seem clingy, but you seem like someone who bathes regularly, and that was something I did specifically ask for in a roommate, so in spite of our obvious differences, I would just as soon you not get kicked out and replaced by someone who likes fantasy but doesn't bathe.

Huh. I had specifically asked for that, too. Maybe the algorithm just ranked priorities differently.

On my way, I texted back.

And then headed straight for the shadows.

***

Another weird thing I'd been doing that summer? Sleepwalking.

My last foster family had agreed to let me stay until college started, but they changed their mind when they found me naked in the backyard one hot July night. I must have gone for a walk and then decided to come home and go sleep skinny dipping— *Now* that's *a bright idea, Remi*—because my hair was full of leaves, and I never even found the pajamas I *know* I went to bed in that night.

Whatever my unconscious reasoning had been, the result was the same. I took one look across the yard at my foster parents' horrified faces, swirling with the pale blue light bouncing off their swimming pool, and I knew they were assuming I'd been up to something much worse. It wasn't worth arguing. I packed my things.

The rest of the summer had been rough, but everything had turned out alright. I was officially a college girl now. My reasonably happy ever after was on its way.

The shadows between the two brick buildings

turned out to be a forest, and when I paused at its edge to study the sign announcing this was some sort of nature preserve cared for by the Environmental Science and Biology departments, with the help of some generous endowments from several fraternities and sororities, I definitely wasn't sleeping.

But I still *felt* asleep. Like I had stepped into one of the bizarre dreams that had accompanied my later summer sleepwalking excursions; the scary ones when I didn't live in a house with other people, but a tent at random campgrounds that cost two bucks a night. The dreams I wouldn't have told anybody about even if I'd *had* anybody to tell because they were so wild, so wacky, so totally un-Remi.

My phone buzzed, but I left it in my pocket as I stepped onto the narrow trail cutting into the woods. My ears roared as my blood began rushing.

Where is it going? I need to follow.

The sky above me had fractured into dozens of darkening blue shapes between a thick canopy of leaves. I ran my fingers over the crooked columns of rough bark lining the trail and wondered if any of them were hickories. If so, maybe I could take a thumbs-up selfie to assure my overeager roommate I was alive and well.

But would that seem friendly, or mean?

My phone buzzed, but when I reached for it, dizziness swept over me like a wave, tipping me forward onto my hands and knees. From that angle, the trail glowed like someone had marked it with fluorescent gold graffiti. *Stupid frat boys.*

Crawling forward, I did have to admit that whatever it was, it smelled amazing. Not like paint at all. Like something good enough to eat.

I licked my lips. My mouth suddenly felt so wet. I'd forgotten to eat. There hadn't been time yet to do any shopping to fill the tiny fridge I now shared with a weirdo named Hickoree who'd probably already stocked it with homemade meals from her perfect home—like leftover roast beef or chicken casserole. I thought about turning back, asking if I could have a bite and return the favor later. I was an okay cook. You learn to make yourself useful when you're borrowing other people's parents.

Oh crap... there's probably a pizza at the sorting ceremony—why am I such a dummy? That's *where I need to be.*

But I kept going. My stomach growled. My head spun. Maybe I was dizzy so often because I wasn't eating enough. All the more reason to keep following the graffiti trail. There was something at the end of it better than pizza, better than chips and dip or leftover casserole.

As I picked up my pace, tiny rocks and pine needles jabbed into my palms and the pads of my feet. I couldn't remember taking off my shoes, but I no longer felt them weighing me down. Actually, I didn't feel *anything* weighing me down. The dizziness was gone. The sweating was gone. My blood had settled in my veins, and I could hear it quietly pumping like a gentle stream. I held my head high and broke into a trot.

Weeds and low-hanging branches brushed my nose and my ears as I followed that irresistible trail deeper and deeper into the nature preserve. My phone hadn't buzzed in forever. Hickoree must have gotten busy meeting all the other nerds who lived for fairy tales. I'd never been happier to be above all that. Real life suited me just fine. Nature, now *that's* where it was at. You never heard Ralph Waldo or Henry David whining because they hadn't gotten their magic school acceptance letters. They were happy with what actually exists.

The graffiti trail led me into a clearing and then vanished. Turning in a circle, I inhaled deeply, trying to pick up the scent. I peered back down the trail to see where I'd missed it, but there was only a still, black tunnel leading back through the trees.

An owl hooted and my muzzle pointed toward the open circle of sky. The stars sparkled like a big city skyline reflected in a river. My ears pricked forward. The whole universe sang. Joy bubbled up from somewhere deep inside me. Joy, but also terrible longing. Loneliness coursed through my veins, but my eyes wouldn't make any tears.

"Sing."

The voice barked inside my brain, but it wasn't mine. My inner voice didn't really sound like anything I could put into words, but this one sounded deep and rich with a friendly sort of twang.

I spun around, hackles lifting, and bared my teeth.

On the other side of the clearing sat two wolves— one black, one white—with their fluffy tails curled politely around their front paws.

The black one looked at me with amber eyes and cocked his head. When he spoke, the words were still inside my brain, but somehow I knew they were coming from him.

"Don't be afraid, Remi. Sing with us."

Then he tilted his head back and howled.

Okay, Remi, time to go. That, I recognized as my own inner voice.

I took several quick steps backward, needing to get back to the dorm, back to the place where normal people like Hickoree lived, where wolves didn't know my name, and the stars didn't sing.

But instead, I tripped over my own tail.

CHAPTER TWO

My butt came down hard on the prickly forest floor.

My bare butt.

Looking down, I found my usual human body and all its associated human parts right where they ought to be, but completely exposed to the hot breeze blowing through the clearing—and the pair of wolves staring at me. I clamped my legs together and pulled my knees up to my chest, while the sane inner voice I'd always treasured so much whispered that this modesty was completely ridiculous since wolves undoubtedly tore the clothes off their victims before consuming their flesh anyway.

"Oh my goodness, I'm so sorry, forgive me," the black

wolf said—still somehow inside my head—and scrunched his amber eyes shut. *"Tell me when you're dressed."*

My mouth fell open.

The white wolf shot the black wolf a look that could only be described as the lupine version of an eye roll. Then it closed its eyes, too.

Okay, yeah, time to wake up. I clenched my own eyes shut and then popped them open as hard as I could.

The wolves were still there, eyes closed and heads politely averted.

"Cherish?" Now the voice in my head sounded female and uncomfortably sexy. *"Do you have this poor girl's clothes for her?"*

"Right here!" Another female voice appeared inside my head, but also somehow behind me, and also... like her mouth was full?

I peeked over my shoulder just in time to see the shape of an upright bear waddling down the same tunnel I had emerged from just moments ago.

My eyes bulged in their sockets. Tremors ran up and down my spine, and my legs turned into useless noodles. *Wake the hell up, Remi!*

I clapped my hands as hard as I could, remembering a long ago camping trip where Foster

Dad #2 told me noise was key in surviving a wild animal attack. But I'd also heard it could work in a pinch for getting yourself out of an unpleasant dream.

But the bear didn't stop. In fact, I think I heard her *laugh?*

She lumbered into the clearing on her hind legs with my T-shirt, jeans, and underwear draped over her awkwardly jutting bear arms while my shoes were stuffed between her massive bear fangs.

She dropped the clothes beside me and settled onto all fours, spitting the shoes out. She smacked her lips and coughed. Strings of drool quivered from her lips but didn't fall. She wiped them away with one truly gigantic paw.

"I'm sorry, sweetie, but I think I swallowed your socks."

I gulped down my heart, which had risen into my throat. "Um, that's okay," I squeaked out. "I have more."

Wow, Remi. Really? This bear could eat you any second and you're not just talking to it, you're lying to it?

The bear backed away, lowering its massive head slightly and averting its eyes.

Still shaking, I snatched my T-shirt off the ground, pulled it over my head, then slipped my bra under my shirt and squirmed into it the hard way. All the while I kept my eyes on the animals, each one with its eyes still closed.

Once I'd wiggled back into my jeans and panties, I tugged my soggy sneakers on and tied them with trembling fingers.

Then I jumped up and ran.

Smack into the once again upright bear's shaggy chest.

A scream rang from my mouth as her powerful arms closed around my shoulders. She pulled me close and began pawing at my back, pressing me into her fur and muffling my cries. They say if you die in a dream, you *really* die. And now that the end had arrived, only one thing flashed through my mind— my brother's face.

Am I about to see him again, or is he still out there?

The bear's diner-waitress drawl came into my mind. *"Honey, I know this is a lot to take in, but let's not do anything rash."*

I fought against the bear, but her paws were too strong. It was no use.

"We only want to talk," the other female voice said in the back of my brain. *"Explain some things that have been happening to you that probably need explaining."*

My thoughts spun. *If I'm not dreaming, I'm crazy.*

And then my knees gave out, and the bear's heavy paws caught me by the back of my head and around my waist, pulling me into—*What the hell? Is this an actual bear hug?*

But for some strange reason, it felt kind of... nice? I'd never thought of myself as being starved for affection, but I must have been wrong because I found myself just going with it. My arms came up and encircled the bear's middle. She rested her lower jaw on top of my head and stroked my hair.

Is this what it feels like to accept your own death? Like coming home from a very long trip you never asked to go on? If so, then farewell, cruel world, I'm ready to go.

I waited for the flash of light, the heavenly choir—surely I hadn't been *too* mean to Hickoree this evening—but nothing changed other than my face getting wet with tears.

"*There, there,*" the bear said. "*It'll all make sense soon.*"

I jerked back.

That's right. I'm Remi St. James. Lover of all things that make sense. And hugging a bear, well, that just doesn't fit.

The black wolf's voice came again. "*What's going*

on over there? Can I open my eyes? Are you decent?"

I whirled around. The white wolf had already opened her eyes, but the black one had stretched out on the ground with both paws over his muzzle.

"Yeah, I'm decent," I said, trying to make my voice sound tough while tensing every muscle in my legs, ready to bolt.

The black wolf sprang to his feet, tongue lolling from the side of his mouth in a friendly canine smile. He bounded over and sat on his haunches in front of me, thrusting out his enormous right paw.

"Hi, Decent. I'm Oberon." He chuckled inside my head like he was just the funniest guy.

The white wolf sighed heavily. The black wolf dropped his paw.

Now I was certain. This was a dream—I mean, of course it was a dream. But it was one of those *Wizard of Oz* dreams where all the wacky characters are really just people you know. The black wolf was a composite of all my dorky foster dads. The white wolf a version of all their long-suffering wives. And the bear at my back... well, she must be that waitress from *Denny's* who gave me extra hash browns that time this summer when I hadn't eaten anything but cold beans for a week.

Okay, whew, glad we figured that out, Remi. Let's just roll with it.

The white wolf stepped forward. *"Excuse my husband. He doesn't know the meaning of 'a time and a place.' Especially in his current state. My name is Cordelia Gladwell, and I am the Vice-Chancellor at the Gladwell Academy."* She gestured with her head to the black wolf. *"Oberon here is the Chancellor. Because, as I'm sure you've already noticed, the world is not fair."*

So that's what this was about. But I didn't need some crazy ass dream to remind me of that. I mean, my parents were so dead I could barely remember them, and my brother—*my twin*—well, nobody had ever wanted us both, so we'd been split up in the system a dozen years ago. We'd found each other online in high school and messaged for a while, but by then we were on opposite sides of the state, and before we'd ever had a chance to meet, he'd stopped answering me. The last time I spoke to my social worker, the day she told me I was on my own now, she finally gave in and admitted that he had run away from a placement gone sideways. As far as anyone knew, *if* he was alive, he was on the streets.

And then there were my own placements that never seemed to stick. They gave me their food and their rooms, but never their hearts, and never the other stuff for long. First, I was too quiet and broody, and then I was too loud and disrespectful, and so on and so on until one day I was just too old. Everyone wanted little kids; the older ones have too much baggage, too many problems.

And didn't I prove them right?

So yeah, the world was most definitely not fair, which I guess is why all the fight went out of me and I sank to my knees in the clearing, eye to eye with the wolves.

"What's happening to me?" My voice sounded small and timid, like it didn't even belong to me. The wolves exchanged looks. The bear's breath fell warmly on my neck, and I reminded myself not to let my guard down too much. We may have shared a moment, but that thing could still eat me if this dream went wrong.

"Why don't we go for a ride?" the black wolf asked. *"Just in case someone's looking for you. Wouldn't want them sending you off to the loony bin for talking to varmints in the woods!"*

"No one's looking for me," I said, but my phone chose that moment to buzz.

"Like I said, let's go for a ride." The black wolf jerked

its head over its shoulder.

"It'll give us a chance to shift into something that makes sense," the white wolf said warmly.

The bear gave me a friendly shoulder bump. *"We're people too, you know."*

***

We emerged from the nature preserve into a rolling hay field. I followed the animals because my subconscious must have crafted this dream for a reason.

Now, to be clear, I didn't believe that dreams contained messages from otherworldly beings or loved ones who had passed, only that dreams had the power to reveal thoughts and feelings our conscious minds didn't know how to deal with. Nothing woo-woo about it—those were just facts. Perhaps in order to launch a successful college career, I needed to address my lingering resentment toward the foster system, or my fear that my brother was dead, or my other fear that he *wasn't* dead but didn't want to know me. This seemed plausible, so I figured I might as well get it over with quickly.

Waiting for us was a long, black limo. The white

wolf touched her delicate nose to the driver's side rear door handle. *"Go on and have a seat. Pour yourself a soda. We'll be along shortly."*

I shook my head in disbelief. *Keep going with it, Remi. You'll wake up soon.*

Opening the door unleashed a cool purple glow, blinding after so much time in the dark forest. Squinting, I ducked inside and slid my butt across the expensive black leather seat, following its curve from the rear door along the passenger side wall. In front of me, between the two driver's side doors, an array of bottles shined purple under the neon lights lining the bar. Above it, where a window ought to be, hung a widescreen TV, showing me what seemed like an incredibly realistic and detailed news broadcast for a dream.

That's so *Remi.*

I picked up a shot glass from the bar and rolled it between my palms. It felt solid and cold, nothing like a dream, but obviously that's what this was. In which case, pouring myself a little something from one of the colorful bottles couldn't hurt. I chose a pink one.

A man poked his head through the open rear door, still buttoning up his pale blue shirt. He smiled at me under a thinning shock of gray-blond hair. "Soda. She said a *soda*."

The black wolf's voice came out of his mouth, but his demeanor was slightly more serious than before.

"Let's try this again." He climbed inside and scooted down the leather seat toward me, right hand outstretched. "I'm Oberon Gladwell, Chancellor of the Gladwell Academy. And you are Remi St. James."

He removed the pink bottle and shot glass from my hands and replaced it with a glass soda bottle from an ice-filled trough in the bar. Then he snatched it back, popped the cap off with some sort of fancy bottle opening gadget, and handed it to me again.

"We usually discourage students from drinking this stuff, too, but no one expects you to quit caffeine cold turkey. Smoking, well, that's another story. Do you smoke?"

I shook my head and took a sip from the bottle, letting the fizzy bubbles work their wonders on my returning headache.

"And no drugs, I hope?"

I stared at him over the upturned bottom of the bottle, and then slowly lowered it. "I'm sitting in a limousine in the middle of a hay field with a werewolf who looks like someone's grandpa, so how about you tell me if I've done any drugs tonight?"

"A grandpa? I don't look that old, do I?" He checked his reflection in the mirror behind the bottles on the bar, pulling at the bags under his eyes and frowning.

"You're avoiding my question, Gramps."

He turned his head sharply. "That's *Chancellor* Gramps to you, young lady."

I raised my eyebrows at him. "Well?"

He settled back on the seat and crossed his ankle over his knee, revealing a thick woolen sock. In *August.* So, *definitely* grandfather age.

"If there are drugs in your system, I can assure you we didn't put them there."

"Well, neither did I."

"Then it seems we're in agreement. Remi St. James is drug free and of a sound mind." He spread his arms wide. "Excellent news!"

Squeezing my eyes shut, I pressed a knuckle into my throbbing temple.

"Deep breaths," Chancellor Gladwell said. "You came out of that shift too fast. Your body may try to go back into it. That's it, nice and slow. Through the nose, out the mouth."

Shift?

As I followed his instructions, the pain lessened—

not completely, but enough to open my eyes when I heard the car door shut. Two women had joined us, each wearing a burgundy blazer over a light blue blouse. The one closest to the Chancellor had brown skin, close-cropped black curls faintly peppered with gray, and the sculpted legs of a woman twenty years younger emerging from under her skirt.

She offered me a finely manicured hand and said in the white wolf's raspy-sexy voice, "Vice-Chancellor Gladwell. So nice to meet you in the human flesh."

My eyes must have been bouncing back and forth between the Gladwells in an embarrassingly obvious manner, because the Vice-Chancellor gave me a patronizing smile as I shook her hand.

"There is no correlation between skin and coat color. It's completely random."

"What color am I?" I blurted out before I could stop myself from asking the ridiculous question.

"Gray." She shrugged. "Like most lycanthropes."

I'm not sure what I'd been hoping for, since I was not a person prone to hoping for anything, but she spoke so dismissively a knot of disappointment formed in my stomach.

Plain. Figures.

"Oh, but she does have those pretty markings around her eyes," the second woman chimed in with the bear's sweet twang. She drew a mask around her own eyes with a fingertip. "Very striking."

That shouldn't have made me feel better, but it totally did. I prided myself on practicality, sure, but that didn't mean I liked the idea of my own subconscious casting me as the dullest character in my own crazy dream.

"Remi," the Vice-Chancellor said, indicating the second woman, "this is Cherish Belhollow, Dean of Science and Health Education at Gladwell Academy. She's also a registered nurse *and* veterinary technician, so she oversees the campus clinic as well."

Dean Belhollow leaned forward, grasped my hand, and shook it vigorously. "It is so, so, *so* good to finally meet you. You've been a hard one to get ahold of!"

"Have I?" I took a nervous sip of soda, nearly spilling the liquid.

The Gladwells nodded in unison.

"We don't normally collect students ourselves," Belhollow went on. "That's the senior-year apprentices' job. But you gave 'em the slip every time. With classes starting in two days, we realized if we wanted it done right, we'd have to do it ourselves."

"Classes?" I set the bottle down on the bar and wiped my wet hand on my jeans. "Classes don't start until next week. This is just orientation for freshmen."

Three pairs of eyes stared at me blankly for a long moment before three mouths burst into laughter.

"Well, not *here*, of course." The Chancellor wiped tears from his eyes. "We're talking about the Academy. Classes start Wednesday. We're going to have to drive all night to get you there in time to register and buy books before the feast."

Feast? That sounds ni—wait, what? No! Focus, Remi!

I waved my hands in front of my face as if clearing a fog. "Buy books? I already did that today. I don't have any money left."

"Oh, no, no, no, honey. The Chancellor misspoke," Belhollow said quickly.

"Not unusual." The Vice-Chancellor smiled wryly.

"No one has to buy anything at Gladwell. It's all paid for." Belhollow patted my knee. "You'll just have to meet with your adviser and drop in on the bookstore. It's really not going to be a problem."

Raking my hands through my hair, I collapsed against the soft back of the seat. Why was I even having this conversation? Why I was still asleep? I drew a deep breath through my nose and let it out through my mouth.

"Good girl," the Chancellor said to me, and then turned to his companions. "She's overwhelmed. Let's roll the tape." He flashed me a proud smile. "We just had it made this year."

I continued the breathing exercise with my eyes shut tightly against the bar's purple glow. There was the sound of old people fumbling with a TV remote and then the whir of a DVD player. A blast of majestic music came close to blowing out my eardrums. More scuffling with the remote, and then the volume plummeted to an acceptable level. I opened my eyes.

The image on the screen soared over foggy mountains decked out in autumn reds and golds, and then dissolved into a wide shot of an enormous stone mansion—castle?—that looked like something from a BBC show lonely housewives watched. Young adults strutted down the sidewalks in the happy, contrived clusters and pairs you'd find in any college's promo material. Similar shots followed: students laughing over pizza in a cafeteria, students playing Frisbee in a courtyard, students pouring over books in a library. All of the things I'd been imagining doing at solid, no-nonsense Keller Park State College for the next four years. If this had all just been some other college's attempt to recruit me, it seemed rather... extreme.

I opened my mouth to say, *No thanks, take me home, my new BFF Hickoree is very worried about me, and I'm definitely in trouble with the R.A.s for missing the mandatory sorting ceremony,* but then a set of broad, muscled shoulders filled the screen. My mouth snapped shut.

The camera zoomed out, revealing the guy's entire shirtless back as his chiseled arms moved through a series of slow motions, like some sort of yoga or Tai Chi. He turned his head to one side, revealing the most perfect human ear I had ever seen, set just above a five o'clock shadow that pulled my eyes down a sharp jawline to a strong chin and enigmatic smirk. Hazel eyes smoldered out from under a swoop of dark, faintly curled hair.

I felt a rush of relief, among other things. This dream was getting itself back to familiar territory. Now if only I could get rid of the talking critters and crack open that screen...

The guy turned his face away, and while there was much to be said for the way his hair brushed the nape of his neck, I wanted the face back. I leaned forward, fighting the urge to touch the screen.

Come back...

The guy began running and the camera followed, never letting the frame drift lower than his lean waist.

Oh, come on! This has been a long, stupid *dream. Help a girl out!*

My future husband—if this dream ever cooperated—picked up speed, every muscle in his back rippling as he crossed a bright green lawn toward dark green mountains. I guess they hadn't shot the video all at once. The camera person probably kept fainting. *I mean, just look at my baby go!*

Suddenly, without missing a step, his shoulders lunged forward and thick yellow fur blossomed down his back as he leapt. When his butt finally rose into the frame, it was covered in fur and sporting a thick lash of a tail. The camera panned down as the mountain lion skidded on the grass, spinning around to swipe at the lens, flatten his ears, and unleash a blood-curdling roar.

Majestic letters appeared over the vicious beast:

GLADWELL ACADEMY OF SHIFTERS.

And then smaller letters underneath:

Where you can learn to be yourself.

The screen faded to black, and so did my brain.

CHAPTER THREE

I awoke to the sound of tires crunching over gravel and glass bottles tinkling against each other. My eyes fluttered open and I stared cross-eyed down the length of my steely gray snout at my moist black nose.

Well, this can't be right.

I sat up on my haunches and scratched behind my left ear with my left foot.

Or this.

My vision felt strange, sharper in some ways, blurrier in others. My peripheral vision took in more than I ever imagined possible. I didn't have to turn my head at all to see the green blur rushing by outside the window over the seat. Even with the heavy tinting, I knew from the way the sun shone a little past straight down that it must be the middle of the afternoon. Ahead of me, through a dark plastic partition over the other curved end of the seat, there were two heads silhouetted in the driver's area.

And to the left, I caught a glimpse of my reflection in the black TV screen. Turning my head fully, I locked eyes with a large gray wolf. And the bear-lady had been right—I did have some very striking markings around my eyes.

I screamed, but it came out as a high-pitched bark.

Why hasn't this stupid dream ended?!

"Good morning, sleepyhead," the Vice-Chancellor's oddly seductive voice came from behind me.

I yipped two more times and tried to spin around on the seat, but consciously moving this strange new body turned out to be more of a challenge than it had been last night when it was doing its own thing without much input from me. My gangly hind legs plopped onto the floor as my front paws scrambled for a hold on the smooth leather seat.

"Please try not to do any more damage, if at all possible." The beautiful black woman from last night sat by the rear door, typing away on a small white laptop. She glanced up and gestured around the space.

"We were hoping you'd sleep all the way there."

My eyes widened and traveled around the limo's formerly luxurious interior. Fluffy white tufts of stuffing exploded from several rips in the leather seating, and a few floated freely around on the floorboard, which I now registered as being sticky and reeking of liquor. Looking up at the bar, there didn't seem to be quite as many bottles as I remembered.

I tried to ask what happened, but of course my mouth didn't work like that anymore, so instead I whined high in my throat, like a puppy.

What the hell, Remi?

"I'm sure you have a lot to ask, but intentional inter-species telepathic communication is an advanced skill you do not yet possess. However, it *is* one you will have ample opportunity to learn as a student at the Gladwell Academy." The Vice-Chancellor closed her laptop and smiled. "While I could easily hurdle your mental blocks, peruse your thoughts, and respond to any pertinent questions, I would rather not violate your privacy again. So, for now, if you wish to chat, one of us will need to shift."

Everything about that sentence should have infuriated me with its nonsense, but seeing as how I had a furry gray snowsuit growing out of my skin, hearing the woman out seemed like the most rational course of action. Unfortunately, I had no idea how to get back into my human skin.

The woman began unbuttoning her blouse.

Um, what's happening here?

"You seem to be a little stuck at the moment, so I'll come to you. You may look away or observe the change. The shame most humans feel with nudity is something every shifter must transcend in due time, but we don't expect miracles overnight."

I closed my eyes, not because I was some kind of prude, but because Foster Dad #4 had been obsessed with hokey old horror movies and if this transformation was going to be anything like some of the scenes in those, I really didn't want to know.

"Ah, that's better." Her voice came into my head a few moments later. *"Now tell me, Remi, how much of last night do you remember?"*

I opened my eyes. The white wolf sat where the woman had just been, next to the laptop and her neatly folded clothes. Her high heel shoes were still on the floor. Climbing back onto my side of the seat, I mirrored her erect posture, curling my tail over my front paws, and thought hard about last night— which was really just a few seconds ago, since of course this was still just part of the same crazy lucid dream I needed to get to the bottom of.

"I remember my dorm, my roommate... feeling like I had to go into the woods, and then following a delicious smell..." My stomach rumbled just thinking about it.

"I apologize for that little sensory trick. We needed to speak to you in a private location, and since your human mind is so... closed, we had to appeal to your animal instincts. Tonight's feast will more than make up for today's empty stomach."

My mouth watered. *"Feast? What feast?"*

"We'll get to that. Go on, tell me what else you remember."

I shook my head and my ears made a funny flapping sound. *"There was a clearing. You were there. A black wolf with dorky dad jokes... Um, a bear? Who ate my socks."*

The white wolf snorted. *"You're lucky you slept through* that *rest stop."*

My tongue rolled out of my muzzle in a nervous pant. *"I know we got in the car and there was some sort of movie maybe, but then..."*

She chuckled. *"But then you became excited by the sight of one of our rare ailuranthropes and shifted on the spot. I hope you can remember the valuable lesson you learned about shifting while dressed?"* She lifted her muzzle to indicate something behind me.

Following her gaze, my eyes landed on the clothes I'd been wearing last night. Someone had gently laid their remains on the other curved section of the seat. My T-shirt was a shredded mess, my jeans two distinct denim tubes. Only my shoes seemed unscathed.

I racked my brain, but couldn't remember anything that went down after the video ended, and the video itself was pretty hazy. A castle. A cafeteria. A library. A guy.

No, Remi, not just a guy. The hottest guy you've ever seen.

Turning back to the white wolf, I asked, *"What's an ailurthroat?"*

"Ailuranthrope," she corrected. *"A feline shifter. Don't be embarrassed. It's not uncommon for them to send lupine shifters over the edge."*

He had sent me over an edge alright, but I'm not sure it was the same one she was talking about.

"A lupine shifter is a lycanthrope. That's you," she went on. *"There are also ursanthropes—or people who shift into bears—like Dean Belhollow. You'll meet all three at the Academy, though wolves make up most of*

our student body."

The Academy. That's what the video had been—a promo to talk me into attending a college full of freaks. As more details came back to me, so did more of my human thinking. I had my life planned out from start to finish, and there was no time to squeeze in a four-year degree in absurdity.

"Yeah, about that... I'm not going."

The white wolf blinked. *"Of course you are. We'll be there within the hour."*

A sharp bark escaped me. I jumped to all four feet. *"What?!"*

"Please sit down, Remi. It's not safe to ride like that, you'll—"

The limo clunked over a pot hole and tossed me into a tangled heap of legs and tail on the floor.

The Chancellor's voice crackled over an intercom. "Everything okay back there?"

"Yes, dear," the white wolf replied. *"Remi is awake. We're having our first advising session."*

"We are?" I asked, staggering up onto all fours. *"Wait, how is he driving?"*

"He's in human form, of course. Dean Belhollow, too. We've been taking turns."

"You don't have a chauffeur?" I asked, because it

was an easy question, unlike all the others bouncing around inside my brain.

"Depends on where we're going and what we're doing. We didn't want too many hands in the pot on this mission."

My head throbbed. I wanted to rub it, but had no hands, so I pressed it against the edge of the leather seat instead. *"Tell them I want to go home."*

"Hmm. And where would that be?"

I glared at the white wolf. That was a low blow. *"I want to go back to my dorm. My roommate's going to be worried about me."*

The wolf thumped her tail dismissively. *"Oh, that's taken care of."*

A low growl rose in my throat. I barely knew her, but Hickoree and her damn magic wands were starting to grow on me compared to all this. *"What did you do to her?"*

"Oh, for Heaven's sake!" The Vice-Chancellor rolled her icy blue eyes. *"We're part-time animals, Remi, not cartoon monsters. After you shifted and began attacking the car, we had no choice but to sedate you. Normally, that would release a freshman shift, but yours held on, so what could we do? Leave you in the hay field and hope you found your way back before the farmer shot*

you?"

"So you kidnapped me?! You could have just waited for me to wake up and then asked what I wanted to do!"

"Time was of the essence, Remi, so we took you into our protective custody," the Vice-Chancellor said firmly. "Don't worry, we have all of your belongings in the trunk. After you were asleep, we found your phone, and Dean Belhollow called your roommate and pretended to be your aunt. She told the girl—what was her name, Oakley?"

"Hickoree. Like the tree. With two ee's. Like a tree," I muttered.

"Right. So, Dean Belhollow retrieved your suitcase and explained to Hickoree that you had a relapse and were being sent to rehab."

"Relapse?! Rehab?! I'm not—I've never!" My brain made the words, but my mouth was making barks.

The white wolf sighed. "Should we have told her you were a long lost princess on an emergency flight home to Belgiastan to claim the throne before your evil uncle could?"

"Yes! She would have loved that!" I spun in tiny frantic circles, as if chasing my own tail. "You didn't need to assassinate my character!"

The limo slowed and then stopped. A moment

later, the rear door opened and the black bear's massive head poked in. Instinct launched me toward the space over her head. If I could just get out of the car, I could find my way—

The Vice-Chancellor knocked me out of the air. I landed on my back, paws flopped over my chest, with the much stronger wolf straddling me. Another instinct told me now was the time to expose my throat.

As soon as I did, she backed off. The limo rocked as the bear squeezed inside, and a second later, the black wolf followed.

"What's going on back here?" he demanded.

"Remi doesn't appreciate the story we—" she gave the bear a hard look *"— told her roommate."*

The bear sighed. *"I'm sorry, sweetie. But that little crayon was sharp. She wasn't going to fall for just anything. I had to make it believable."*

I rolled over onto my stomach, facing away from all of them. I didn't know who to be angrier with. These creatures that had kidnapped me, or myself for making the kind of first impression on Hickoree that would make it easy for her to believe I was some sort of troubled addict.

"Where is my phone? I need to text her right now." I

didn't care if I didn't have thumbs, I would figure it out.

"Your phone is still in your jeans pocket, but I'm afraid there's no signal out here. You'll have to wait," the white wolf said.

"'Til when?" I groaned.

"Our winter break starts the day before Thanksgiving..." the black wolf offered cheerfully.

I jumped up and spun around to face them again. *"Are you saying I can't tell anyone where I really am until Thanksgiving?!"*

The black wolf tilted his head and kind of shrugged. *"Well, technically, you can* never *tell anyone where you are..."*

A series of guttural grunts and snarls erupted out of my jaws, and while they didn't have exact translations into English, I somehow knew these were not sounds young wolves should make in front of their mother... or to school administrators.

Suddenly weirdly embarrassed, I turned away from them and dropped to the floor with my paws over my nose. *"Sorry."*

"Remi, my dear girl," the black wolf said in a fatherly tone. *"We know this can't be easy for you to understand, but you* are *a shifter, and shifters* must

attend an Academy."

"*It's not safe out there on your own,*" the bear—Belhollow—said.

"*You must learn self-control if you ever wish to lead any kind of life among other humans.*" The white wolf gently nudged my ear with her nose. "*We can teach you those skills, and so much more. And, in time, you may even come to see that being a shifter means never being without a family.*"

Family. Did she really think that sort of sentimental—

Family!

My claws scrabbled against the floor. I spun around, unable to stop the wag in my tail. "*My brother! Have you found him yet?*"

The animals exchanged glances. The white wolf tilted her head. "*Your brother?*"

"*Yes!*" I did a puppyish spin in the tight space between the bar and the seat, kicking up a whirl of white stuffing. "*My brother! Rahm! My twin! If I'm a shifter, then he must be too!*"

The looks on their faces carved all the joy out of my heart and splattered it on the floor. My tail drooped. My ears fell flat against my head.

"*I mean... right?*"

Belhollow touched my cheek ever-so-gently with her claws. *"I'm afraid it doesn't work like that, baby girl."*

"There is no genetic component," the Vice-Chancellor said carefully. *"The chance of two people in one family—even twins—being shifters... well, it's astronomical."*

"Shifting is a gift, Remi," the black wolf chimed in. *"Given at random."*

My haunches sank to the floor. *"Then why didn't you give it to someone who would want it? Like Hickoree. She'd be all over this."*

The Chancellor shook his head. *"The gift is not within our power to give, or to take. You are what you are, Remi. All we can offer you is the knowledge needed to embrace it."*

"But my brother... he's been missing. What if he's looking for me? And he tracks me down at Keller Parks, but Hickoree tells him I've gone to rehab, and he's looking all over the place while really I'm just stuck in—I don't even know where!"

Overwhelmed by the emotional roller coaster of this stupid, never-ending dream, I threw back my head and released a mournful howl.

Instantly, the other two wolves joined me, our

voices filling up the limo and leaking out the open door into the vast forest beyond. Again and again and again, we howled, and as we sang, my pain became their pain, and I felt flashes of their own, of children dreamed of but never born, of the sorrow that drove them to build a school where the strange and lost never had to be alone.

Our song faded. Outside, birds chirped and bugs droned and the leaves rattled and the tree trunks creaked, but inside, no one spoke, not for a long time. The other animals seemed to be communicating with each other now on a channel I wasn't tuned into.

Finally, the bear cleared her throat. *"This brother of yours, honey... He can't attend the Academy, of course, but perhaps—"*

"Yes, perhaps," the black wolf nodded. *"If you come willingly..."*

"And work hard," the white wolf said sternly.

The black wolf smiled, showing off his glistening fangs. *"We could send a team of trackers to look for him."*

And that was how I, Remi St. James, patron of all things reasonable and sane, voluntarily enrolled in werewolf college.

CHAPTER FOUR

We pulled up alongside a five-strand stretch of barbed wire fence tacked onto a line of half-rotten wooden posts and draped in a thick layer of kudzu vines. Belhollow—human again—hopped out of the passenger seat. Pressing the side of my head against the window, I could see her up ahead, fiddling with a simple chain and padlock on a rusty metal farm gate. It swung inward with a squeal that sent a sharp pain through my sensitive wolf ears.

The limo made what seemed like an impossibly sharp right turn through the opening and kept going, leaving Belhollow behind to shut and lock the gate. We didn't go far. Another sharp right turn and the limo stopped, engine idling, waiting for Belhollow to catch up. I knew we must be parallel to the dirt road we drove in on, but it had vanished behind a thick copse of cedar on our side of the fence.

Good thing this is all just a dream my mind has cooked up to deal with my family abandonment issues, or this would be getting really spooky.

I took a deep breath through my nose like the Chancellor taught me, and released it through my mouth, which caused my long pink tongue to flop out and a drop of saliva to splash onto the leather seat.

Gross, Remi.

And then the bouquet of aromas my powerful nose had gathered without my conscious effort washed over my brain like a wave on sand, leaving behind the black-and-white image of an enormous wooden barn nestled among the trees. I yelped in surprise—not because it was a brand new experience for me, but because it was most definitely *not.* Only, I'd never had any context for understanding it before. I had always told myself I was just really good at reading people and situations and making educated guesses based on facts—like when I knew what Hickoree had in her boxes—but now I'd discovered the unsettling truth.

I can see *with my nose. What the actual hell?*

Belhollow smiled and wiggled her fingers at me

she passed by the window. But instead of getting back in the car, she walked toward the barn ahead of us. A moment later, she rolled back what sounded like a massive wooden door hung on an ancient metal track, and the limo drove into the dark belly of the barn.

A whine squeaked out of my throat, and I stamped my paws on the seat, spinning in a tight circle. I scrambled over to the rear door, not caring that the Vice-Chancellor's legs were in the way. She laid a gentle hand on my head.

"When I open this door, your instincts may compel you to run into the woods, but you must ignore them and stay with us. Do you think you can do that, or shall I put a leash on you?"

A leash?! Yeah, that's not happening.

I growled and pawed at the door.

"Very well. But know that if you run, I can shift and catch you faster than you can blink. But I would rather not destroy these clothes, if it's all the same to you."

She cracked the door an inch. I rammed my muzzle into the opening, forcing my way out, and bolted for the square of green-hued light at the front of the barn.

A strong hand caught the scruff of my neck and

hurled me backward. I rolled three times in the dirt and hit my head on the edge of something metal. I let out a sharp yelp.

"Oberon!" Belhollow exclaimed. "That was a little much!"

Shaking my head clear, I looked up. The Chancellor seemed a lot larger than he had inside the car. His face softened and he knelt in front of me, holding out the back of his hand like you would to any old dog.

"I'm sorry, Remi. This old *gramps* forgets his strength sometimes. Are you okay?"

Dazed, I touched my nose to his hand. He smiled and ruffled my right ear. Then he stood up with a grunt and walked around me.

The Vice-Chancellor emerged from the limo with a laptop case slung over one shoulder. She lifted her eyebrows at me. "Rule number one: No shifting between the inner and outer perimeters without written permission from an approved faculty member. You'll get your chance to explore when you're assigned to a patrol."

Patrol? Is this college or boot camp?

I stood on wobbly feet and looked around. The limo rested in the center aisle behind a heavy-duty farm truck streaked with mud. To the right, a towering block of square hay bales filled the area where the stalls would have once been, and to the left waited a small convoy of UTVs.

Belhollow moved our luggage from the limo's trunk to the small open bed of the closest UTV. Then she patted its tiny tailgate and motioned at me. "Up! It's a bumpy road and the seat belts aren't made for animals."

I growled to indicate I did *not* appreciate being treated like a pet, but I also really didn't want to get tossed around again, so I obeyed.

Ugh. Who's a good girl, Remi?

The Gladwells slid onto the UTV's front bench, and Belhollow took the second. Turning in a few circles as the engine revved up, I tried to get comfortable among the hard edges of our suitcases. So far, the prestigious Gladwell Academy of Shifters was not looking quite like the elite lifestyle advertised in the promo video.

***

After a harrowing fifteen minutes weaving between trees that grew so close together I didn't see how a rabbit could squeeze through, much less a speeding vehicle shaped like a box, we emerged at the foot of a brilliant green meadow gently sloping up to a gray stone wall coated with emerald green moss. Four spires reached for the sky from somewhere behind the wall, shining like dark fangs against the blue-tinged mountains rising in at least three layers behind the campus.

Now that's more like it.

As we began our slow, rattling ascent, Belhollow pressed her face against the grate between us and shouted over the engine, "Listen, sweetie, I just want to warn you. The atmosphere at Gladwell is competitive, to say the least. Most freshmen can't hold a shift longer than an hour or two, so your condition may cause a ruckus. But there's no way for us to force an un-shift, so you'll just have to grin and bear it until it wears off on its own. In the meantime, be prepared to deal with some jealousy."

Jealousy? Am I back in high-school?

The wooden gates swung open when we reached the top of the hill, and suddenly our tires were rolling quietly over smooth cobblestone. The driveway cut through a vast manicured lawn and looped around a cascading fountain topped with three bronze statues—a wolf, a cougar, and a bear.

The three-story building from the promo video loomed over everything, looking less like a posh British manor up close and more like an Ivy League dorm had a half-evil baby with a haunted mansion from a Gothic horror story. Neat hedges lined the sidewalk, and a couple of guys played Frisbee on the lawn, soaked in the eerie shadow of the spired tower rising one floor above the rest.

"Therian Hall!" Belhollow announced, and then lowered her voice as the engine cut off and we parked. She hopped down and opened the tail gate, pulling out my suitcase and her own. "Here we go!"

I glanced over my shoulder at the Gladwells, who were deep in conversation in the front seat.

"Oh, they don't live here, honey." Belhollow leaned into my ear and muttered, "They've got their own little mansion between the perimeters."

Hmm. Maybe she's not so immune to jealousy herself.

I jumped down to the cobblestone, and the Gladwells drove off without so much as a backward glance. My tail drooped.

No parting words of wisdom?

And then I heard the first snicker.

You know that dream where it's the first day of

class and you've showed up naked? Well, that's what kind of dream this abruptly turned into, except instead of being naked, I was the only one wearing a fur coat. Belhollow had tried to warn me, I supposed, but still, I'd expected at least a few other students to be in their animal skins.

Nope, turned out I was the *only* one standing on all fours with her tail between her legs. And the only one everyone else was suddenly staring at. *Laughing* at.

Belhollow waved her arms at the onlookers. "None of that! Let us through."

The crowd parted, but then most of them followed us under the arch into the covered porch before the true entrance. Off to the side, two steps led up to a glass door with words my wolf eyes couldn't decipher, but the shelves stuffed with books gave me a clue.

"That's the bookstore," Belhollow told me, looking like a crazy lady talking to a pet. "Closed now, but there'll be time before class tomorrow to get what you need."

She led me up a wider set of steps where three pairs of doors stood wide open. We went through the center pair and emerged into an enormous space full of round tables draped in pristine white tablecloths, each one bearing an elaborate centerpiece made from antlers and flowers.

Whoa. Is this what geek girls like Hickoree mean when they describe something as a Great Hall?

Sunlight streamed through three stories' worth of windows spanning the entire width of the cavernous room. At either end, balconies on the second and third floors allowed students to gaze down on the activity below. Above it all a gold and crystal chandelier dangled from a vaulted ceiling painted to look like a blue-green night sky.

Beyond the bank of windows, an impeccably landscaped courtyard lay nestled between the two wings of the building that extended backward from either side. Each wing was dotted with smaller windows overlooking the gravel paths and strands of warm yellow lights that snaked between the small trees.

"This way, baby girl." Belhollow jerked her head to the right, and I stayed close to her heels, trying to ignore dozens of whispering mouths and wandering eyes. "Women over here, men over there," she went on. "You'll be on the second floor with all the other freshman and sophomores. Juniors and senior are on the third. Classrooms are on the first."

"New pet, Dean?" a meaty jock with a full beard asked as we walked by.

"New student, and I would appreciate it—" she spun around then to snarl at the entire room "—if you would all show her some *respect* and go back to whatever it was you were doing before you all started acting like you've never walked on four legs before."

The crowd behind us shrank back under the force of her glare. She eyed every single person in the room before pointing at a gorgeous, curvy, blond girl attached to a preppy but not particularly handsome guy.

Money talks, Remi. Even to animals.

"You there. Come here," Belhollow ordered.

The girl pointed at her chest and looked around innocently.

"Yes, you. I want you to show Miss St. James to her room. 2G, I believe." She held out my suitcase. "Help her with this, too."

The guy next to the girl laughed, and she elbowed him in the ribs. Her lip curled in disgust. "What am I? A bellboy?"

"You're a *guest* receiving an all-expenses paid education, so chop chop, little lady. Do as you're told."

The girl huffed and flounced over. She ripped my suitcase from Belhollow's hand, dropping it in the process. I winced, thinking of the framed photos inside.

"Oops. I'm sorry, *Miss James*." She feigned a curtsy in my direction.

"What's your name, girl?" Belhollow demanded.

"Winter Davenport," she replied, like it meant a lot wherever she was from.

"Well, Miss Davenport..." Belhollow smiled. "I look forward to seeing you in Health and P.E. Thursday. Twenty laps should take you down a few notches."

Winter's pale face turned blood red as she snatched my suitcase off the ground and spun away. Looking up at Belhollow, I turned on the saddest puppy eyes I could muster. *Please don't make me.*

Belhollow shooed me away. "Go on. I've got my own freshening up to do before the feast."

"Are you coming, James?" Winter snarled over her shoulder.

I barked sharply. *No one leaves out the Saint.*

Belhollow waved like she was sending me off to kindergarten, and then disappeared through a sturdy door to the left of the arched entrance to the stairwell.

The moment the door closed, the entire student body erupted into howls of laughter. I rotated in a tight circle, wondering if this was how dogs and cats felt all the time, surrounded by towering two-legged creatures with bald faces and gaping maws emitting nonsensical sounds.

Winter dropped my suitcase for a second time and strutted away. She glowered down at me with the sort of petty hatred I hadn't felt from another girl since that time I spilled fruit juice on Patricia Serrano's white jeans and everyone called her Period Patty for the remainder of freshman year.

Okay, maybe that wasn't *so petty of Patty.*

"I don't take orders from ugly bears," Winter sneered, tossing her blond locks over her shoulder as she passed by.

Rage boiled over in my animal brain. I lunged, teeth snapping at Winter's perfect posterior. The room tilted suddenly, and bile rose in my throat. For a split second, the world went black, and then my human nose slammed into the hardwood floor.

Pandemonium broke out. Girls were screaming, guys were whooping. I lifted my sore face off the floor just in time to see Winter's guy high five his far more attractive buddy. Winter punched him in the chest, but probably not out of any sense of sisterhood.

I couldn't move. For one thing, every inch of my body felt like jelly, and for another, every inch of my body was stark naked. I could live with everyone seeing my ass, but the up-front stuff was between me and my mirror.

"Oh, you think you're really something, don't you, James?" Winter called, face contorted with a level of rage that told me she had some deep issues I shouldn't take too personally.

Tossing tendrils of hair out of my eyes, I snarled back, "*Saint* James."

She scoffed. "Did you hear that, Derek? She thinks she's a saint! But would a saint do a strip tease for half the guys on campus?"

A cool breeze whisked by me and then a soft cloth settled over my body. A hand reached down to me, and a female voice said, "Ignore her. She's just mad because she can't do a flying shift either way."

I let the hand lift me off the floor, clutching the tablecloth tightly around me as I stood on shaky legs. The girl in front of me had flawless light brown skin and glossy black hair pulled into a pony tail. If the muscles bulging in her arms had belonged to a guy, I would have been very attracted to them.

"Victoria Manuel. And you're Remi St. James, I know. Nice to finally catch you." My face must have shown my confusion because she grinned and said, "I spent half my summer vacation trying to bring you in, but you were *not* having it."

"Oh. Um. Sorry?" I tucked a strand of hair behind my ear.

She shrugged. "Got me out of going to my sister's fourth baby gender reveal party, so you and I are totally cool. I mean, once you've found out you're a shifter, it's hard to feign shock and awe over the color of a cake. Did I mention it was the *fourth* time?" She picked up my suitcase. "Where are we going?"

I laughed politely at her story. "Um, 2G maybe? I can carry that."

"It's cool, I've got it. You're probably feeling a little unbalanced, yeah?"

I nodded. She slid her arm around my shoulders as we made our way up the stairs to the second floor, and that was honestly the only thing keeping me from tumbling backward down the steps.

"Good news is private rooms. Bad news is public restrooms." She jerked a thumb at a door as we walked by just in time to hear a toilet flush.

"At least there's *something* normal about this

college."

Victoria laughed. "You'll get used to everything else. Promise. It's pretty cool."

"What year are you?"

"Senior, so you probably won't see too much of me."

Damn it. Now I have to try to make another friend in this circus?

"But," she went on, "if you want, you can sit with me and Laith at the feast tonight. No one will give you any trouble with us."

"Laith?" I asked, wondering what the hell kind of name that was.

"Yeah, my boyfriend," she said quickly, dropping her arm. "You *might* like him. He's an acquired taste."

"I'll like anyone who isn't named after a season at this point."

"You're funny, Saint James." Victoria stopped in front of a wide wooden door bearing a little golden plaque that read 2G. "See you at the feast."

CHAPTER FIVE

Therian Hall's 2G was three times the size of the concrete cube I should've been in with Hickoree, but every luxurious inch belonged to me. A queen-sized canopy bed took up the center of the room, with royal blue drapes tied to each of its four posters, framing a mountain of pillows at the top of an absurdly thick duvet. Matching blue curtains framed the view of the actual mountains rising up like blue-green waves ready to crash over the stone wall.

I dropped my suitcase next to the enormous wooden armoire to the right of the door and gawked at the tiny kitchenette on my left. A granite counter-top held a stainless steel sink and a toaster oven, with a mini fridge built in underneath. Two chairs waited on either side of a small table set with two full place settings. I opened the fridge and found an army of designer water bottles standing at attention.

The floor shone with a recent re-finishing, but there were still faint scratches visible in the smooth wooden planks. I crossed to the living area under the window, running my fingers along the foot of the bed as I went. The room's right corner contained a plush sofa and sleek coffee table, both angled toward the flat-screen television hanging on the wall directly across from the bed. In the left corner, a heavy, roll-top desk sat between two ornate bookcases. The shelves were empty, but when I opened the desk, I found a shiny white laptop like Vice-Chancellor Gladwell's.

I sank into the desk chair, letting the table cloth fall from my shoulders, and relished the ice cold air-conditioning blowing on my bare skin after a whole night and day stuck in a fur coat. My scalp itched wildly, and my right foot frantically tapped the floor until I clamped my hand on my knee.

Be normal, Remi.

I used my trusty human hand to tend to the itch, then forced myself to my feet, leaving the table cloth draped over the chair.

First order of business: getting clean.

Second order of business: getting dressed.

Third order of business: staying that way.

I figured I would just wear my pajamas to the restroom, but standing in front of the armoire, I caught another one of those strange mental whiffs and saw a fluffy white robe in my mind—right down to my name embroidered over the chest pocket.

I flung open the armoire doors. The robe dangled from a wooden hanger, its sash tied in a perfect bow at the waist. I stroked the lapel, unable to remember ever touching anything so soft. My fingers moved to the right, tracing the blue thread spelling out my name.

Goosebumps erupted on my arms, and not just because people shouldn't be able to see hidden objects with their noses. In the limo, I had agreed to enroll voluntarily if the Gladwells agreed to look for my brother, but there was no way someone had sewn my name onto this robe in the hour or so that had passed since then. The robe had been ready and waiting, which made me wonder...

What if I *hadn't* said yes?

***

Forty-five minutes later, I leaned my elbows on the second-floor balcony and searched the faces at the tables below me for the one I wanted to find—Victoria's—and the one I wanted to find even more—Winter's. She needed to get a look at me now in my trusty lace-up boots, strategically ripped skinny jeans, and loose black V-neck top paired with two silver chains and my favorite stingray-shaped bracelet.

The community bathroom had not been anything like the hellscape poor Hickoree was stuck with back at Keller Parks. Each toilet stall here had a solid wooden door, and the showers were made of stone tiles just rough enough to provide traction for the funny plastic socks we were supposed to pull over our feet to avoid spreading any fungus. The tiny, hotel-style bottle of shampoo nestled in a carved-out cubby had restored my gnarled rat's nest of hair into something soft and silky and—yeah, okay, I'll brag—sexy as hell.

Bring it on, Davenport.

I spotted her bright blond hair at a table in the center of the room—of course—surrounded by the same group she'd been with earlier: the preppy guy and his handsome-yet-brutish friend, plus three other girls. From this distance, they appeared to be sitting next to Winter in descending order of resemblance. I charted the course I would need to take to catch the boys' eyes. Not because I was even remotely interested in either of them, but because I didn't need a wolf in me to know that you're lunch if a girl like Winter smelled fear. My first move after such extreme humiliation had to be one of absolute confidence.

Closing my eyes, I practiced the Chancellor's breathing exercise a few times, willing all the fibers in my body to stay like they were right now. Then I tossed my newly glossy waves over my shoulder and strutted down the stairs like I owned not just this campus, but the whole damn Smoky Mountains. I could have sworn I heard my personal soundtrack swelling in the background, rocking the kind of song I'd put on a playlist called *Swagger*.

But somehow the stairs jumped up to meet me halfway down the first section, and I went cart-wheeling through the air and face-planted on the landing between floors, narrowly avoiding a collision of my boot heels with the majestic window overlooking the dusky front lawn.

My mental music screeched to a halt.

So much for my movie montage.

"Someday I'll meet you on your feet, but looks like today is not that day."

I rolled over, untangling my face from my previously perfect hair, and looked up at Victoria's friendly smirk. Once again, her hand was reaching out to me.

"Anything broken yet?" she asked as she pulled me to my feet.

I swept my hair back over my shoulder. "Only my pride."

"You're ahead of the game then." She smiled. "Makes the professors' jobs so much easier if you're already broken on the first day of class."

I laughed nervously. "That tough, huh?"

"Tougher than walking downstairs with your boot untied, anyway." She pointed at my feet. "Better fix that."

I groaned and re-laced my boot. *Properly.* "I promise I'll be a normal person tomorrow."

She laughed. "After tomorrow, you're never going to be a normal person again."

"I've gotta be honest," I said as we descended the second section of stairs, "that's pretty much the last thing I want to hear."

Victoria chewed her lip thoughtfully. "I get it. I wasn't wild about being here at first, either. It's like, it was bad enough—well, I already had a lot going on." She shook her head as we stepped into the Great Hall. "But once I learned to control my shifts, I never looked back. What we are, Remi, it's *amazing*. Lean into it. Stop telling yourself it can't be happening. It is."

Ha, nice try, brain! But you can't fool me with this older, wiser character. I know this is a dream.

We walked alongside the row of windows facing the courtyard, my mission to teach Winter a lesson aborted. The sun had sunk far enough behind the mountains for the lightning bugs to come out and dance among the twinkling strings of light hanging between the trees. Dark shapes moved along the sidewalk and laughter filtered around the edges of the heavy double doors we passed. At the next window, I caught a glimpse of two silhouettes entangled on a bench, seemingly trying to gnaw each other's faces off.

Not literally, I hope.

Glancing around, I realized that almost none of the students gathered at the tables underneath the brilliant chandelier were paying any attention to us. Not even the ones we were sliding around and scooting by were throwing shade my way.

Guess nobody recognizes you with your clothes on, Remi.

"There's Laith," Victoria said, and I followed her pointing finger to a table up ahead, empty but for one male figure with his back to us.

My heart, liver, and intestines immediately started trying to rearrange themselves. I dug my fingernails into my palms and ground my teeth.

Don't do it, Remi. Don't you dare.

Even with his clothes on, I recognized that back. He wore a gray dress shirt with the sleeves rolled up to his elbows, revealing his long, sinewy forearms. Dark tendrils of hair flirted with his collar, and when he turned his head, his lips wore that same enigmatic smirk from the promo video.

"Hey, babe," Victoria said when we reached him, resting her hands on his shoulders and pecking him on the cheek.

Well, this is an unfortunate plot twist.

"Hey, *babe*," he replied, rolling his eyes. They caught on me, and he shifted, cocking one elbow over the back of his chair. "What the hell, Vic? Didn't I say no dogs until we have our own home?"

"Excuse me?" I snapped, bristling at his casual insult, not to mention sexism.

"He means you're a wolf, not a, you know, *woof.*" Victoria made an ugly face over her shoulder as she took the seat next to him. "But he still shouldn't judge people by their animal."

"I don't," he scoffed. "I judge animals by their people."

His voice had a southern lilt, not a twang or a drawl, just enough of an accent to make him sound like he probably knew how to fix a tractor or gentle a horse in whatever life this school had dragged him away from.

Fix a tractor? Gentle a horse? What the hell is my subconscious into?

He stuck out his hand. "Laith Brighton. And you are... wait, let me guess. Wind Runner? No, no, Night Crawler! Or maybe Moon Walker?"

Victoria jammed her elbow into his side. "She hasn't been here long enough to even get your stupid speciest jokes. Could you *try* being nice?"

"It's okay," I said, gripping Laith's hand.

Huge mistake. A prickling sensation swept up my arm and across my shoulders before spreading down the rest of my body. Like I'd fallen into a mound of fire ants and not only were they stinging me, they were injecting me with electricity.

I yanked my hand back, leaving his hand hanging awkwardly in the air. He stared at with a quizzical, almost comical look that made my heart shrivel up with embarrassment. *What if he felt my fur trying to worm its way out?*

"And it's Lion Tamer, actually," I blurted, frantic to distract him. "My name."

He dropped his hand and his smile skewed to the left while he bit the right corner of his lower lip. "You'll have to bring your whip next time."

Heat rushed up my neck. *Oh, good job, Remi. If you're going to flirt with a guy in front of his girlfriend, just go ahead and make it kinky. Why not?*

Victoria grabbed my wrist and dragged me around to the chair on her other side. "Like I said, an acquired taste."

I sank into the chair, keeping my eyes on the place mat in front of me, but I sensed Laith leaning around her to look at me.

"But seriously, who are you?"

"Remi," Victoria answered. "Saint James."

"Oh," he said knowingly. "*You're* the one."

Of freakin' course.

"Yep, that's me." I glared at him. His right elbow was propped on the table, making all the veins stand out in his wrist in a way that made me hate him because the alternative to hating him was now strictly forbidden. "Remi the Stripper. First show was free, next time I expect tips."

His hazel eyes danced behind his swoop of hair. He began counting off on his long fingers. "One, I have no idea what you're talking about. Two, I am certainly intrigued. And three, I was referring to the fact that you held a beginner's shift for eighteen hours. True or not true?"

"I mean, yeah, I guess," I stammered. "Wait, who's saying that?"

He shrugged. "I heard Belhollow telling Mardone."

Oh, no... what if Belhollow told him what brought on my marathon shift?

"Who's Mardone?" I made myself ask instead of blurting out an apology to Victoria for getting so worked up over her boyfriend that I literally lost control of my body.

Victoria laughed darkly. "Lenore Mardone, Dean of Liberal Arts Education. She's got enormous—" She made the universal gesture for a large chest. "And she's not afraid to rest them on a cute guy's desk. Total cougar."

Laith shot Victoria a withering look. "So are you, *babe*."

Victoria shot one right back. "You know what I meant, *honey.*"

They held each other's glares for a long second until they cracked up.

Ugh. If the one thing I actually wanted out of this dream was going to make me a homewrecker, I was more than ready to wake up now.

Victoria turned back to me. "Laith is her hand-picked T.A. this year."

"Wow," I said. "That sounds like an honor."

Laith snorted. "I guess."

Victoria rolled her eyes. "He's just grumpy because he'll have to be nice to so many wolves at one time."

"Oh, well, don't strain yourself on my account," I told him curtly. "There's nothing I hate more than a cat walking all over my desk while I'm trying to work."

That was supposed to be a jab, but it only made him smile that adorable smile again. "What about when it swishes its tail all over your face?"

I lifted my eyebrows. "That's when I throw it out the door."

Victoria guffawed at that and gave me a high five.

Laith scowled at her. "Are you forgetting yourself?"

There was this weird, like, nanosecond where Victoria looked stricken, but it passed in such a flash that felt like I must have imagined it.

Victoria shrugged. "Gender before species, dude."

Someone tapped on a microphone, making it squeal. Every student in my line of vision cringed and covered their ears.

"Sorry, yes, this thing is on," the Chancellor's voice boomed through the Great Hall. A hush fell over the crowd. "Hello everyone! Wow. Look at all of you. So many good-looking faces. Even the bears. Who knew?"

Everybody laughed. Even the bears, I guess. Apparently it was a thing. I shifted in the direction they were all looking. The Chancellor stood in front of the courtyard doors, holding a microphone. He looked almost dashing in his burgundy jacket with his hair tamed back behind his ears.

"Listen, I'm going to keep this short because

we're all hungry, and I don't want another incident like '08. So much paperwork." He groaned and slapped his forehead, earning more laughs.

Victoria touched my arm and said, "He's joking."

"Tomorrow I expect everyone to show up for class, ready to work hard and become the best beasts you can be." He paused for a cacophony of human howls and growls. "But tonight, we feast! Let's give a big round of applause for the upperclassmen who brought this bounty home! I hear we have venison from the wolves—"

A group of older-looking students pounded on their table and howled.

"Salmon from the bears—"

Another table exploded with banging fists and heavy grunting.

"And, holy cow, am I excited about this... Our mountain lion has brought us an elk!"

Laith waved lazily at what seemed like a rather grudging round of applause.

"Whoa, settle down over there, Laith. You're getting too worked up," the Chancellor joked, but Laith just turned back to the table, sneering.

"What is he talking about?" I whispered to Victoria.

But before she could answer, a cart loaded with lidded dishes rolled up beside Laith, pushed by a young server with a sort of vacant look in his eyes. Glancing around, I saw other servers with other trays alongside the table with the wolves and bears we'd just applauded.

"I'm shutting up now, but remember..." the Chancellor said, and then the entire student body joined in as he finished, "Tradition. Transition. Transformation!"

I swore the building shook with the force of their applause. I clapped my hands together too, of course, but felt incredibly lost and more than a little creeped out. I had never been much for group chanting.

The server beside Laith whipped off one of the silver lids, revealing a plate loaded with brown and pink hunks of meat. There were veggies, too—steamed asparagus and roasted potatoes—and some buttery rolls, but when the smell of the game hit my nose, I nearly blacked out.

Victoria gripped my arm and whispered, "Stay with us. Breathe."

In through my nose. Out through my mouth. Victoria's fingers dug into my skin, grounding me in this body. The world came back into focus.

She patted my arm and smiled. "Don't worry. It happens to the best of us."

I shook my head and swallowed the embarrassing amount of saliva collecting in my mouth. "What is all this? What was he talking about? I am like... so lost."

Laith was already tearing chunks of meat off what appeared to be a rib in his hand. I simultaneously wanted to fight him for it and throw up.

The server slid a plate in front of Victoria. My stomach growled wildly.

Victoria started cutting up a slab of salmon with her knife and fork. "Every summer, the junior and seniors—well, some of them, I was rounding up freshmen instead—they go on a hunting trip and—"

My plate landed in front of me just as I nearly jumped out of my chair.

"Everything okay, miss?" the server asked blandly.

"I'm fine, thank you." I waved him away and whipped my attention back to Victoria. "A *hunting* trip?"

Laith looked up from his plate and snorted. "What? Don't tell me you're a vegetarian."

"No, I just..." My eyes trailed down to my plate. The slab of salmon. The set of blackened ribs. The fried venison medallions. I had never craved anything so desperately, yet I could never allow myself to eat them. Tears stung my eyes.

"What the hell? Is she *crying*?" Laith muttered, and Victoria shushed him.

"I can't... I mean, I don't..."

I am so hungry.

Victoria touched my shoulder. "What is it? What's wrong?"

"I don't believe in hunting," I blurted.

Laith laugh—no, he *guffawed*. He dropped his rib on his plate. "You don't believe in hunting? But you eat, like what? Burgers and chicken nuggets and crap?"

Frustration closed up my throat. "No," I squeaked. "I try to eat healthy..."

Laith stabbed one of the medallions on his plate. "Doesn't get any healthier than this. No hormones. No processing."

"Yeah, but... listen, I'm sorry, I don't want to be rude, I'm just not cool with hunting. It's not fair."

He dropped his fork and gaped at me. "And you think a cow has a sporting chance?"

I dropped my head into my hands, fighting the urge to bury my face in my plate. "No."

"Well then," he resumed his bite. "You don't have a problem with hunting."

Anger welled up inside me. I slammed one arm on the table and leaned around Victoria to glower at Laith. "Yes, I do. I have a problem with grown men dressing up like bushes and sitting beside a watering hole with a gun—"

He laughed with his mouth full. "*That's* your problem?"

My jaw twitched from the effort of not lunging at him. "Yeah. *That's* my problem."

He leaned forward, mimicking my position. "Well, you're in luck, Poodle." He held up the rib. "Because I killed this guy with my *teeth*."

CHAPTER SIX

Remi St. James, Gray Wolf
Freshman. Semester One.

> **Intro to Therianthropy: Fact vs. Fiction**
> **Professor Daniel Helms**
> **M/W 1:00 PM – 2:30 PM, Therian Hall 101**
>
> **Exploring the Mindscape**
> **Dean Lenore Mardone**
> **M/W: 3:00 PM – 4:30 PM, Therian Hall 113**
>
> **Wolf Music I (No Credit, Required Extra-**
> **curricular)**
> **Chancellor Oberon Gladwell**

W: 9:00 PM - 12:00 AM, Amphitheater

Health and Physical Education for Shifters
Dean Cherish Belhollow and Dean Gareth
Embry
T/Th: 1:00 PM - 2:30 PM, Shiftnasium Room
A

Practical Shifting I
Dean Gareth Embry
Th: 9:00 PM – 12:00 AM, Shiftnasium Room
C

College Writing I
Self-Paced, Online

I stared at the piece of paper Vice-Chancellor
Gladwell had just slid across her desk. The words
appeared to be written in plain English, yet only two-
thirds of them made any sense.

"Is there a problem?" the Vice-Chancellor asked
in the sort of pleasant tone people only use when they
really don't want there to be a problem.

"Yeah. I can't wake up," I muttered.

"We do have a coffee shop. Did no one tell you?"

She lifted her paper cup like she was giving a toast.

Groaning, I buried my head in my hands. "That's not what I meant."

The Vice-Chancellor sighed and set the cup back on its coaster. She folded her elbows on her desk. "I realize my official title can be intimidating, but as your personal advisor, I'm here to listen to any concerns you might have regarding your classes, professors, or peers."

I glanced up through a cascade of my own hair. *Is she trolling me?*

Smoothing my hair into place, I leaned back in my chair and gestured at her office. The walls were covered in paintings and tapestries of wolves and humans transforming into wolves. Even the rug beneath my feet had wolves running around its border. An enormous set of antlers hung on the wall behind the desk, positioned just high enough so that no one could poke their eye out on one of its many tines. A small nameplate on the polished wooden plaque holding up the mount read:

Cordelia Hollins, 1980 - First Kill

"My concern is that I've experienced almost two

whole days inside a dream." I glanced out the window at the mountains trapping me here. "Where is the real me? Am I in a coma?"

The Vice-Chancellor tilted her head. "Remi, do you still not know this is actually happening? You *are* the real you. You are right there in that chair."

Tears burned at the edges of my eyes. I wanted to go home. I wanted to be getting to know that weirdo Hickoree. I wanted to be flipping through the pages of all the text books I had already bought at the bookstore. I did want coffee, but I wanted it from the food court in the Keller Parks student center, a nice, plain building with no chandeliers or scalloped white plates piled high with wild game I could never bring myself to eat. I didn't want to have shown my ass to the entire student body, and I didn't want to feel my body bending itself into or out of the shape of a wolf. And I really, really, *really* never wanted to see stupid Laith Brighton's smirking face again.

The Vice-Chancellor steepled her fingers. "Your brother. What was his name again?"

"Rahm." I sniffled. "R-A-H-M." No one ever spelled it right.

She picked up a marbled pen and scribbled that down. "St. James also, yes?"

"Yeah. I mean, yes, ma'am." I rubbed my stinging eyes with my wrist. "But he could be going by something else?"

She lifted an eyebrow. "Any ideas what that might be?"

I shook my head and shrugged. "I barely even know him."

She smiled warmly. "Well, hopefully we can fix that. Do you have any pictures of him?"

"No. Not recent ones. But he does have some social media profiles. He doesn't use—"

"Ah! Excellent." She scribbled something else down, and then gave me a very serious look. "Remi, students at Gladwell Academy are entitled to perks you won't find at very many other colleges. For starters, it's free. You'll never owe us or anyone else a dime for the time you spend here, and that's only the beginning of what we have to offer, Remi. But, as nice a girl as you seem to be, we can't help you with anything like finding your brother if you aren't attending the Gladwell Academy."

She leaned across the desk and pushed the bizarre schedule closer to me until it teetered on the edge. I snatched it up before it could hit the floor.

"The Shifter community is small in the grand

scheme of things, Remi. Our resources may be large, but they are still finite. We simply can't spend money on shifters who aren't willing to buckle down and do what it takes to become productive members of our society. Maybe we weren't clear enough about this yesterday, but do you understand what I'm saying?"

I started folding the paper into tiny squares. "Take the classes or never see my brother again."

"My goodness, Remi. You make it sound like blackmail." She laughed and shook her head. "But you're the one who asked. We're only trying to help you here."

"I understand," I mumbled, and then quickly added, "Thank you."

"You're welcome." She tapped the paper she'd scribbled on. "Now, why don't you run down to the bookstore to get your books while I get started on this?"

Nodding, I climbed to my feet and picked up my empty book bag. "Do I just show them my schedule or what?"

"Yes. Ms. Shirley will know what you need."

I made myself return her smile, and then carefully walked over to her office door. My body felt like it had...well, turned into something else and gotten stuck that way for almost an entire day, and then spontaneously re-appeared stark naked in front of pretty much everyone at my new college.

Just as my hand touched the knob, the Vice-Chancellor called out, "One more thing, Remi."

Turning back, I found her standing with the paper bearing my brother's name in her hand. She came around the desk and touched my shoulder.

"I noticed you were sitting with the mountain lions last night. I understand there was an incident and Victoria offered you some assistance, but don't forget to make friends with your own kind, too." She gave me an encouraging pat on the back. "Freshmen packs form quickly, and you won't want to be left out."

My own kind? As far as I could tell, my own kind was more than willing to engage in social cannibalism, while the lions—well, *one* of the lions— had been nothing but supportive and kind. The other lion could kiss my ass right along with Winter Davenport and the laughing hyenas she ran with.

But it didn't seem like a point worth arguing, so I pretended that I would follow her advice, thanked her one more time, and slipped out into the stairwell that occupied one corner of Therian Hall's tower. The

Gladwells' offices occupied the top floor, while the Deans shared the third floor, and the rest of the faculty were apparently squeezed into the second. All three office suites were accessible only through the attic of the bookstore that sat snug against the tower.

The glass door chimed as I entered the attic, which seemed to be purposefully decorated with cobwebs, given the intense levels of luxury and cleanliness I'd found everywhere else in the building. A rickety banister lined the opening to the stairs. My boots sank into the plush purple carpet as I descended the steps that wound around the book-stuffed walls. There were the books you'd find in any campus bookstore— *Catcher in the Rye, To Kill a Mockingbird, Infinite Jest*— but there were also plenty of books that could only be described as frightening and weird, such as *Between Shifts: A Memoir of a Hybrid Life.*

That would be just my luck.

On my way up, the store had been crowded with students buying last minute supplies, but it appeared to have emptied out after the lunch bell. When I reached the first floor, there didn't even seem to be anyone there to man the counter by the front door where the open sign stilled glowed bright red.

"Who goes there?" The female voice quivered

with age.

I startled and grasped the banister. "Um, Remi? St. James?"

The voice mumbled my name a few times, and then a head popped up over the counter, sniffing the air. "You haven't received your books yet."

I shook my head, but then realized the tiny woman couldn't see me. Her eyes were as white as two small moons. "No, ma'am. I just arrived last night."

She clapped her gnarled hands together. "How exciting! And here I thought I'd gathered my last book batch for the season." She reached out over the counter. "Well, come on, show me your schedule."

Unfolding the piece of paper, I stepped over to the counter. Up close, I could tell she was standing on a stool. The skin around her moon-colored eyes folded over on itself in what seemed like hundreds of tiny wrinkles. She patted the marble counter top with one liver-spotted hand.

"Here is fine."

"Um, okay," I said. "Do you need me to—"

But the woman held up a hand to silence me. She bent her head, touched her nose to the paper, and inhaled deeply. She smiled. "Of course. The freshman usual."

My jaw dropped. Was this some sort of parlor trick, or could she see things—*read* things—with her nose, too?

"I'm Ms. Shirley, by the way." The woman hopped off her stool and came around the counter. She wore thick-soled granny shoes and a frumpy purple sweater that most people wouldn't need for another two months at least. But I suspected there wasn't a scrap of meat on this lady's bones. She had to be pushing ninety, at the very least.

Hopefully shifters don't age in dog years, Remi. This might be you in ten years.

I suppressed a shudder and followed Ms. Shirley as she moved briskly around the store, pausing now and then to sniff a shelf and add a book to the growing stack in her arms. Finally, she led me back to the first floor, slid my books onto the counter, and hopped back up onto her stool.

"This is my favorite part of the job. Of course, it's pretty much my whole job. Not many students come visit once they've got what they need from me."

"I'll come visit," I blurted without thinking.

Her mouth dropped open and her blank eyes grew wide. "That would be *so* lovely."

Then her nose started twitching and she waved

her head back and forth across the counter.

"Um, Ms. Shirley? Can I—"

She held up her hand. Then she snatched a stamp from the far-left side of the counter. She held it up like a prize. "Got it!" She began opening my books and stamping their inside covers.

"Ms. Shirley?"

"Yes, dear?"

"I'm confused. Is this a bookstore or a library?"

She stamped a book titled, *You, Your Body, and Your Other Body.*

"Well, I suppose it's both. You don't have to pay for anything, but you don't have to bring anything back either."

"Oh. Well, what's the stamp for?"

She smiled at me, revealing several gaps in her teeth. "It's a special scent marker. To make sure none of these books wind up in the wrong hands."

Somebody howled outside. I peered out the glass door and saw Winter's boyfriend—what was his name again? Derek?—and his henchman wrestling on the lawn, while Winter and her three minions watched and squealed.

Oh, great.

I glanced at the clock behind Ms. Shirley. Twelve-thirty. Half an hour to go before my first class. I had intended to find the coffee shop, but maybe I'd just hide in here for a little while.

"Ms. Shirley, can I ask you something? I don't want to be rude."

She sighed and slammed my last book shut. "You want to know what happened to my eyes. Well, none of your business."

I flinched. "No, ma'am. I'm sorry. I just wanted to know if... well, when you're sniffing things? Do you just know their scents, or can you see them?"

She chuckled. "I can't see a damn thing, dear."

"No like... inside your head?"

Her face paled. She glanced from side to side and leaned over the counter, almost crashing her nose into mine. "Why would you ask that?"

Swallowing hard, I moved my face away. Her breath smelled less than fresh.

"Well, it's just that sometimes... for example, last night in my room, I was standing in front of the armoire, and I caught this whiff of something, but it wasn't a smell I could put into words." I bit my lip nervously. The old woman had begun to tremble. "But somehow I could see that there was a robe inside. I even saw that it had my name on it."

"Oh, child," she murmured. "Oh, child. Come closer."

I leaned in, hoping she couldn't see-smell my grimace.

She put her lips right up against my ear. "You must *never* tell this to another soul."

I jerked back. "What?"

She shook her head from side to side. "A terrible gift. Terrible. Tell *no one*."

"A terrible gift?" I fought back the urge to grab her hunched shoulders and shake her. "Are you saying I'm cursed?"

What? You don't believe in curses, Remi. Or gifts, for that matter. Snap out of it!

Ms. Shirley jumped down from the stool and backed up against the wall. Tears welled up from her sightless eyes, and she pressed a finger to her lip. "Shhhh. Tell no one what you know."

"Ms. Shirley, *please*!" Anxiety prickled my skin. "You have to tell me!"

"No, no, no..." she moaned. "Oh, child. You must go."

"Go where?" My voice cracked.

Ms. Shirley gave her head a vigorous shake. Her gapped smile returned. "Why, to class, of course! Off with you now!" She pointed at the door. "Don't forget to come visit!"

My breaths came in short gasps. My heart pounded inside my chest. Sweat trickled down my chest as I took several steps back. Ms. Shirley waved placidly, which was somehow even more terrifying than the cryptic episode I'd just witnessed.

I gathered my books off the counter and dumped them into my bag, but when I reached for the door, I found soft gray hair sprouting from my skin.

Oh, shift.

CHAPTER SEVEN

"Oh no, child, you can't shift in here," Ms. Shirley scolded, scrunching her nose.

"I'm not *trying* to!" I shouted, backing away from the glass door with my hairy arms stretched out in front of me.

My whole body itched as fur blossomed beneath my clothes. I writhed, fighting the urge to rip my shirt and jeans off while I still had hands to rip with.

"What do I *do*?" My voice cracked like a yelp on the last word.

Winter and her pack were still goofing off on the lawn, and there was no freakin' way I was giving them the satisfaction of seeing me like this. White hot pain seized my limbs, and I doubled over against the counter. The room went black and I heard my stack of books tumble to the floor.

"Upstairs!" Ms. Shirley shouted.

I scrambled blindly for the stairwell, somehow still on two legs. My guts roiled like a nest of snakes as I felt my way haltingly up the steps. By the time I could smell that I was reaching the musty attic, my teeth had grown to sharp points in my mouth.

Two strong arms caught me by the shoulders and lifted me the rest of the way up the stairs, my legs kicking at the air. A moment later, the slamming of a door echoed in the faculty stairwell. The unfamiliar hands pressed me against the wall.

"Shh, shh, hold still, darling." The man had a posh British accent. "You're experiencing a slow shift. I'm going to need to place my hands on your head. Do I have your permission?"

My head flailed, but I couldn't tell in what direction.

"Right then," the man said. "I'm going to assume that was a yes. Feel free to slap me when you have your hands back, if I'm wrong."

The man shifted his weight so his body held me to the wall while his hands encircled my head, fingers pressing into my skull, palms covering my ears, thumbs stretched across my forehead. Warmth washed over my short-circuiting brain and poured down my neck and over my shoulders, loosening every contorted inch of me until I slumped against the man's hard chest.

"Sorry!" He let go of my head and gently pushed me back against the wall. "All right, darling?"

My eyes blinked into focus, and the second most handsome face I'd seen on campus filled my vision. Stunning blue eyes radiated concern beneath a gently furrowed brow. His tousled blond hair glistened like a halo around his clean-shaven face. I felt my mouth curling into a stupid, dreamy smile.

That voice... and those manners! Here's a guy who deserves being crushed on.

And then I remembered where I was—the *faculty* stairwell.

I jumped, bumping my head on the wall. He jumped too, lifting his hands like I was a cop.

"Please don't slap me, I only meant to help."

Rubbing the back of my head, I groaned. "I'm not... I know... but what did you *do*?"

"Reverse shift. Simple mental procedure. Sorry about the, ah..." He wiggled his fingers. "Hands."

"Dude, it's okay," I said, pushing off the wall and

looking down at my totally human, still clothed, body. And then I cringed. "Oh, god, I'm sorry. You're not a dude..."

"Well, technically..." He tilted his head and flashed his dimples.

"I mean, you must be a professor. Maybe even a dean. You could be a doctor for all I—" *Stop rambling, Remi.* I closed my mouth.

"Professor, and a very low-level one at that." He bent to pick up a leather satchel. "On my way to my first class now. Might I escort you down, or did you have further business up here?" He twirled one finger upward to indicate the spiral stairs.

"Um, no... I mean yes..." *Get it together, Remi.* "I only came up here because of the, uh, the hair." I hugged myself self-consciously, realizing how lucky I'd been not to lose any clothes in front of this very attractive, very polite, very kind, very *young* professor... *who is just another product of my own subconscious and not an actual authority figure it would be wildly inappropriate to have a crush on.*

"Well, then, shall we?" He held open the glass door. "Do you have a class now?"

"Yes, it's... I can't remember the name, um..." I searched my pockets for my schedule, but then realized I'd left it downstairs with Ms. Shirley and my books. "Werewolves 101?"

He threw back his head and laughed. "Werewolves 101. Oh my. That's marvelous."

Blushing, I scrunched my head into my shoulders. "Or something."

"I think you mean Intro to Therianthropy." He touched me lightly on the shoulder. "It appears we'll be facing our first class together."

A pleasant tingle radiated from the point where his fingers brushed my skin. Nothing at all like the ferocious prickling that came when I touched Laith. Maybe this dream wasn't a lost cause yet.

***

There are probably worse things a girl could do for her reputation than walk into a class five minutes late with a professor whose face belonged on the Most Eligible Bachelor issue of *Shifting Style* magazine—if such a thing existed—but not when the only remaining desk in said class was right next to Winter Davenport.

My butt had barely touched the chair when she leaned across the narrow aisle and whispered, "You don't waste any time booking private shows, do you, James?"

"*Saint* James," I hissed. "I'm not trying to be pretentious. That's just what it is."

Winter opened her mouth, but the professor cleared his throat, and her head immediately snapped to the front.

So she's an overachieving *mean girl. Duly noted.*

"Good afternoon, and welcome to..." the professor smiled, clearly trying not to chuckle, "Werewolves 101."

Two nerds in the front row guffawed, then shrank into their seats when nobody else joined them. The professor glanced my way and gave a tiny shrug. I would have shrunk into my seat, too, if it wouldn't have made his implication that we shared an inside joke even more obvious. But from the corner of my eye, I saw Winter's lip twitch, and I knew she'd picked up on it.

Wonderful.

"You know some of us are bears, right?" a voice growled from the back of the class.

Glancing over my shoulder, I saw Derek's hunky pal turned sideways in his desk so his legs could violate the personal space of the girl sitting next to him. I tried to offer her a look of sympathy, but she quickly buried her nose in her open textbook.

So that's how it's going to be.

The professor smiled. "Yes, of course I know that. It was merely a joke. A bit of an icebreaker, if you will. Apologies if I've offended, Mr.... what is your name?"

"Chad Tyson," he answered through a yawn.

The professor pulled a pen and piece of paper out of his satchel and made a quick mark. "Chad Tyson, present. Right then, let's go around the room. Name and animal, please."

The class turned out to be split two-thirds between wolves and bears, with no mountain lions at all. I didn't know if all lion guys were as off-putting as Laith Brighton had turned out to be, but I felt relieved to be free of them all the same.

"Excellent. All present and accounted for." The professor set the attendance list aside and clapped his hands together. "Now let's—"

"Sir?" Winter raised her hand. "You haven't told us yours."

He smacked a hand to his forehead. "I'm so sorry. Of course you'd want to know that." He cleared his throat. "I am Professor Daniel Helms, a gray wolf, and I am a graduate of the Hawtrey Academy of Great

Britain."

A surprised murmur rippled through the class.

"Yes, there are Academies on every continent except Antarctica." Helms said as he moved around his desk to the blackboard. "We'll actually discuss them briefly in this class when we go over the different international shifter species later this semester, but they will be covered in-depth in History of Therianthropy in the spring. Now, who can tell me what that word means?"

"History?" Chad grunted.

Ignoring him, Helms wrote *'Therianthropy'* in large, neat letters on the board. "Come now, anyone? Don't be shy."

One of the front row nerds raised his hand.

Helms pointed. "Yes, Kanze, was it?"

Kanze nodded. "Therianthropy is the ability of a human to physically transform into an animal, but..." He looked down at his desk.

"But?" Helms prompted.

Kanze swallowed. "But if you go online—"

"Ah." Helms lifted a hand. "Let me stop you right there, because that is a can of worms that we will be opening in a few weeks. Today, I want to focus on the *historical* definition of therianthropy, which is, as you said, the ability of a human to physically transform into an animal."

Helms moved to another section of the blackboard and drew a cross.

"Now, I am sure that until very recently, most of you believed therianthropy to be pure myth. Most of what you know—or think you know—about the subject will have come from books, movies, television, comics."

In the top left corner of the cross, he wrote '*FACT*' and in the top right corner, he wrote '*FICTION.*'

"The purpose of this course," he continued, "is to help you sort through the most basic misunderstandings, rumors, and outright lies surrounding our unique ability. I'd like us to go around the room one more time, and share one thing pop culture taught you about therianthropes."

Over the next twenty minutes, we learned that no, shifting is not caused by the full moon, but that the belief may have sprung from true shifters being spotted on brighter nights; we learned that yes, silver bullets *can* kill us, but only by virtue of being, you know, *bullets*, and not because they're made of silver; we learned that, likewise, the wolfsbane plant is wildly poisonous, but not somehow more poisonous to us; and we learned that no, biting someone would not give that person the ability to shift, it would just give them a nasty bite and be considered "quite rude."

By the time my turn came around, the few things I'd gleaned about werewolves over the years from horror movies and blabber-mouthed fangirls had already been covered.

"I'm sure you can think of something," Professor Helms encouraged after I had awkwardly explained that I'd never really been into this sort of thing.

When he smiled at me, his dimples appeared for the first time since we'd been alone in the stairwell, and my palms began to sweat. I rubbed them roughly on my jeans.

"Um, well..." I stammered, heart pounding in my ears, racking my brain for anything else one of my foster sisters might have said over the years. A memory flashed across my mind, and before I could think twice, I blurted out, "Do werewolves mate for life?"

The whole class snickered, and I felt my ears glowing red. But to make matters worse, it appeared my question had also made Professor Helms blush.

He swallowed hard and tugged at his tie. "Ah. Well. Actually, there is a bit of truth to that one."

A hush fell over the room.

Helms scratched the back of his head. "It's not... I mean, there's no loss of free will. Relationships do go south, and mates go their separate ways. Mine certainly did." He laughed, and then looked adorably, heart-breakingly mortified. "Goodness. That was awkward. My apologies." He cleared his throat. "But, ah, yes, in general the tendency toward monogamy is, shall we say, more pronounced among wolf shifters than other species."

Chad whooped and slammed his hands down on Derek's shoulders in front of him. "Dude, I told you to slow your roll! You're done for!"

Derek shrugged him and reached back as if to slug him. "It's not like that!"

Casting a sideways glance, I noticed Winter had joined me in the bright red ears club. I had just started to feel sorry for her when her head snapped to the right and she pinned me with her icy blue eyes.

"Well, I guess you didn't waste any time locking down those A's, did you, James?"

CHAPTER EIGHT

My book bag landed on my desk with a heavy *thunk*, followed shortly by my forehead. I folded my arms over my head, rubbing out the knots of tension this day had left in the back of my neck.

And it's not even over yet.

I thought about crawling back into bed, burrowing under the covers, and refusing to move until I woke up back in the real world, but it hadn't worked last night, so I didn't have any real hope that it would now. Something had happened to the real me—of that, I was certain, regardless of what the Vice-Chancellor or any of these other dream people wanted me to think—and until that Remi woke up, this Remi was apparently going to be a student of the Gladwell Academy of Shifters.

The question was... *why?*

Glancing up through a curtain of messy hair, my eyes found my brother's in the framed family photo on my desk. The glass in the lower right corner was cracked, and while I couldn't say for certain it hadn't happened on the way here, I was pretty sure I had Winter dropping my suitcase to thank for that. If I weren't so sure the real version was safe and sound back in my dorm with Hickoree, I might have let my wolf out to snack.

I had no memory of the photo shoot, but the low-res fireplace backdrop told me our parents had taken us to one of those cheap places in a mall. All four of us were decked out in cheesy matching Christmas sweaters, me on our dad's lap, Rahm on our mother's. My tiny reddened face looked unimpressed with the level of nonsense underway, but Rahm's eyes danced with mischief, and his grin was borderline maniacal. I'd been carrying this picture around for thirteen years, waiting for a chance to ask my brother if he remembered what the photographer had been doing to elicit such different reactions.

The Vice-Chancellor might not be blackmailing me exactly, but she was obviously using my brother as a bribe to get me to stay.

No, not *stay*. Leaving was clearly *not* an option. It was a bribe to get me to play along. To pretend I was some sort of werewolf—excuse me, *lycanthrope*.

On the one hand, it hardly seemed worth it. Finding my brother here wouldn't be any different from all the other reunion dreams I'd ever had. Eventually I *would* wake up, and he'd still be missing.

But on the other hand...

What if the reason my subconscious had concocted this particular dream was to guide me to some long lost knowledge hidden deep inside myself that could help me solve the mystery of my brother's disappearance in the real world?

With a resigned groan, I emptied my book bag onto the desk. There were a handful of normal books for the writing class I'd be taking online, plus four remarkably abnormal titles. Aside from *You, Your Body, and Your Other Body*, there was the book for Helms' class titled, *It's Not the Moon, It's You*, and then two workbooks full of journaling prompts and other odd activities, one titled *Practical Shifting I* and the other titled *Exploring the Mindscape*.

I looked at my phone to check the time—the only thing it was good for now. It had zero bars, and no way to tap into the Academy's network. The isolation was more than a little unnerving, but also understandable. If some random person's leaked nudes could go viral, imagine if someone sent out pics of a student in mid-shift.

It was 2:45. I slipped *Exploring the Mindscape* back into my bag, thinking I probably ought to get there early lest I accidentally give Winter the satisfaction of seeing me walk in with Dean Mardone too. Swinging the bag over my shoulder, I took one last look at the family photo, at my parents tired yet proud expressions, at my brother's joyful grin.

I can do this. For Rahm.

***

Laith Brighton looked up from the ring of flat cushions he'd been arranging on the hardwood floor. That stupid, lopsided, lip-biting grin crossed his scruffy face, and the only thing that saved me from spontaneous transformation was the abrupt realization that he'd come to class in his pajamas.

Made of hemp, my nose somehow informed me.

"Well, well, well." Laith folded his arms over his chest, just under his shirt's deep V-neck. "If it isn't my favorite new house pet."

I blinked. "Why are you wearing pajamas?"

He looked down at his loose, cream-colored shirt and pants and lifted his palms. "I'm not?"

"And where the hell are the desks?" I demanded, gazing around the mostly empty space. Blackout curtains were drawn, and the only light came from candles flickering on small tables around the edges of the room. The smell of incense assaulted my nose and some chime-y, ting-y music threatened to make me rip off my own ears.

Laith swept his arms out, indicating the cushions. "Right here, Poodle."

"Don't call me that," I growled, dropping my book bag next to one of the mats.

"Whatever you say, my little Bichon Frise," he purred, brushing past me with such indifference that I could have sworn I felt the ghost of a feline tail tickle my nose.

"What is all this?" I tried again for some kind of explanation as to why I had walked into a yoga studio, not a classroom.

"Romantic dinner, can't you tell?" He sidled past me again, carrying another armful of mats. "Me, you, candles, music... maybe a little elk?"

My skin prickled like a million tiny hairs were

trying to wiggle their way out, but I clenched every muscle in my body, refusing to let them. I would never give this arrogant ass the satisfaction of knowing even his faux flirtation made every cell in my body go haywire.

"You okay there, Yorkie?" His eyes raked me up and down. "You look a little... constipated. Why don't you sit down?"

"You're disgusting, you know that?" I crossed my arms and planted my feet, refusing to actually sit on one of the ridiculous cushions. "How did you manage to talk someone like Victoria into going out with you?"

He snorted as he dropped the mats. "Our relationship is taking place as per her request."

"I don't even know what that means."

"It means, Miss Maltese, that *she* asked *me*." He kicked the mats into position. "And having no better offers at the time, I agreed."

"Ugh." I shook my head. "Does she know you talk about her like this?"

He opened his mouth, and then paused, letting out a pained sigh before he asked, "And what was it she told you about me?"

I smirked. "She said you're an acquired taste."

"Well, there you have it." He bowed his head so his hair swung across his eyes.

Those eyes. Hazel with golden flecks that danced in the candlelight. A wave of heat washed over my face, momentarily rendering me speechless.

Remi, you're swooning.

Stop swooning.

Right now. Stop it, Remi.

You would never go after another girl's boyfriend.

No matter how gorgeous his eyes are.

Oh, and also? He's a total jerk. Snap out of it!

"But seriously, what is all this?" I finally said out loud and gestured at the room again. "Are we having a séance or what?"

He rolled his eyes. "The class is called Exploring the Mindscape. What do you think this is?"

I lifted my arms and raised my eyebrows like, *You tell me.*

He mimicked my gesture, but with a mocking edge. "It's a meditation class? Obviously?"

A scoff jumped out of my mouth. "Are you kidding?"

He nudged the cushion nearest his toe. "Well, it's not nap time."

"Unbelievable." I combed both my hands through

my hair, tugging on the strands. "I thought we were at least *pretending* this was some kind of real college."

The amusement left his eyes. A wall came down over his features, hardening them. "Do you have a problem with meditation?"

I laughed, a little too maniacally. "Don't *you*?"

He shook his head. "Meditation is the first step in making space to know our own minds." He stepped closer, his voice fervent. "And until you know your mind, you can't control it, and until you can control it, you'll keep shifting in and out of your skin at the most inopportune times."

Oh crap. Does he know what he does to me?

"Wow." I held my ground, even though I wanted to melt into the floor, and something sizzled in the small space between us—the white-hot electricity of mutual disdain, I supposed. "I did not peg you for the woo woo, crystals and spells type. What with all the blood thirst."

"Funny." He arched an eyebrow. "That's *exactly* what I had you pegged for. What with all the bleeding-heart crap."

We glowered, both of our lips curling, and though I wasn't shifting, I could still feel all the hairs lifting on the back of my neck.

If his face weren't so handsome, I'd rip it right off.

"Laith, what's going on here?"

He practically leapt backwards at the sound of the woman's voice. I turned to see someone who could only be the infamous Dean Lenore Mardone standing in the doorway, one hand on its frame, the other on her ample hip. She was in her early thirties at most, with a fountain of hair that held all the colors of autumn leaves and a figure that stretched every limit of the faculty skirt and blazer in ways even I had to admit were... flattering. But the way she wore her light blue blouse significantly less buttoned up than either the Vice-Chancellor or Dean Belhollow added an off-putting air of desperation to the ensemble.

She frowned at me, but her words were clearly meant for him. "Is there a problem?"

"No, Dean Mardone." His voice took on an extra layer of southern charm. "We were just, uh, playing a staring game."

She lifted one perfectly sculpted eyebrow and chuckled, but she didn't seem all that amused. "A staring game?"

I heard Laith swallow behind me. "You know, when you see who'll look away first?"

Mardone squinted at him for a moment, then

burst into a true laugh. "Against a *wolf*!" She gestured at me dismissively. "Well, I hope you were winning, kitten."

Kitten? I had to bite the inside of my cheek not to laugh. *That'll put him in his place.*

Shaking her head, Mardone flipped her wrist at him like, *You silly old thing.* "I'll be in the little girl's room, freshening up. Everything looks fabulous, Laith. You're going to be just what I needed this year."

I could hear his teeth gritting when he said, "I aim to please, Dean Mardone."

She rolled her eyes. "Oh, please. If I've told you once, I've told you a thousand times. I want you to call me Lenore." Her eyes snapped to me. "Not you, of course. Go ahead and take a mat. Let Laith do his job."

Mardone breezed back into the hallway, and the second I was sure she was gone, I spun around, laughing so hard I had to put my hands on my knees.

"*Kitten?*" I wheezed.

Laith stalked over to the supply closet, a vein in the side of his neck throbbing. He stormed back and threw three more mats onto the floor at my feet. "You think sexual harassment is funny?"

My laughter died in my throat. I straightened up and awkwardly cleared my throat. "I'm sorry. I didn't think—"

He snorted. "Typical wolf."

"Hey!" I barked. "I said I'm sorry, okay? You don't have to be such a jerk."

He waved me off, turning away. "Sure thing, Poodle."

Seething, I grabbed his elbow and yanked him back around. "Don't you think that's a little hypocritical of you?"

He rolled his head on his shoulders and groaned. "What is?"

"Calling me pet names when—"

He threw his head back and laughed. "Girl, these aren't pet names. They are *insults*." He drew the last three words out like I was stupid. "Don't flatter yourself." And then, for good measure I guess, he spat, "Poodle."

My hands balled up into fists, just as the hallway roared to life with footsteps and voices. I unclenched them and struck my best impression of Dean Mardone's sultry posture. "Whatever you say... *kitten*."

Laith's lips drew back in what sounded like an honest-to-goodness hiss, but before I could be sure, Winter Davenport appeared in the doorway, stopping her pack of jackals in their tracks. Her blue eyes darted between me and Laith, highlighting the very short distance between us.

Her mouth fell open. "*Kitten*? Seriously, James? Are you cheating on Professor Helms already?"

Red hot rage clouded my vision like blood at the scene of a shark attack, which was fitting since that's the sort of black-eyed killing machine I would have guessed Winter actually had inside her. My wolf strained against every muscle in my body, from my little toes up to my tongue, demanding release.

And why shouldn't I knock this witch off her broom? Someone needs to.

And so I relaxed the chokehold I'd had on my body ever since Laith flashed his stupid dimples at me.

Come out to play, girl.

Nothing happened.

The sensation swelled until I was sure I would come apart at the seams, but then, abruptly, the wolf shrank back, leaving me with only the hollow feelings of confusion and defeat.

"Did you just try to *shift* on me?" Winter shrieked. "What kind of psycho *are* you?! Where is the Dean? Derek!" She clutched her boyfriend's arm. "Go get the Dean!"

He looked from her to me and back again, even more dumb confusion than usual etched across his brow. "I didn't see—"

Winter shoved him. "Just go, you idiot!"

He winced, but obediently backed out into the hallway, leaving space for the three minions to slip into the room and huddle protectively around Winter.

"You're just lucky Winter didn't shift," the one who looked the most like her sneered.

"Yeah, she would have eaten you alive," the second one said as she rubbed Winter's back.

"And I would have helped!" shouted the least attractive one, and by least attractive I mean she would have had to settle for being a print model instead of a catwalk model like her friends.

Winter sniffled for the benefit of her companions. "That is the second time she's gone after me. When Dean Mardone gets here—"

"She'll ask her teaching assistant what happened," Laith said, appearing at my side. "And he'll tell her Remi was provoked by some dumb dog who thinks student-professor relationships are a fun rumor to start."

Winter gasped. "*What* did you just call me?"

"You heard me. Now sit down." He pointed at the

mats. "All of you."

Winter crossed her arms. "I don't take orders—"

"You most certainly do, Miss Davenport," Dean Mardone said from behind her. "Laith is my right hand man in this class. You will show him the same respect you show me."

"But James..." Winter started.

Mardone waved her words away as she walked to the front of the class. "I don't know who that is, but if Laith isn't concerned, I'm not concerned. Take your seats."

Icicles shot from Winter's eyes as she walked past me, but she led her pack to the mats at the back of the room, as far away from Dean Mardone as she could get.

I turned to Laith, prepared to swallow my pride and thank him, but before I could even open my mouth, he shook his head and walked away, muttering, "Just sit down, you little Shih Tzu."

My fists curled at my side, and I counted slowly to ten, partly to cool my temper, and partly because I refused to obey him. It took every one of those ten seconds to talk myself out of walking right out the door. The only thing keeping me here was my brother's face, smiling out of the cracked picture frame.

For Rahm, I reminded myself as I sank onto the stupid mat.

Dean Mardone tapped a tiny mallet against a small gong on one of the candlelit tables. "Let's begin. Laith, will you please shut the door?"

Laith bowed his head and walked to the door with his hands clasped behind his back like some kind of butler. The soft *click* of the door latching into place sounded to my ears more like the heavy *clang* of a prison cell closing.

"Welcome to Exploring the Mindscape," Dean Mardone said. "For those of you who don't know yet, my name is Lenore Mardone, and I am the Dean of Liberal Arts Education. In this class, we will focus on a variety of meditation techniques drawn from an array of ancient traditions..."

My eyelids fluttered with the gentle flickering of the candles on the walls. The music was totally hokey, yet also kind of soothing to my frayed nerves. I swallowed a yawn. *Do they seriously expect me to stay...*

"Remi St. James?"

I startled awake. "Yes? What? I'm here."

Mardone scowled down at me over the clipboard in her hands. "Miss St. James, in this class, it is not enough to be non-absent, you must be *present* as well."

"Yes, ma'am," I mumbled, shaking the nap fog out of my head. "I'm sorry."

Sorry I got caught.

Mardone gave me a tight-lipped smile. "Apology accepted. *This* time."

She moved on, calling out the handful of names between S and Z. When she was satisfied everyone was non-absent, she handed the clipboard off to Laith, who then faded into the shadows in the corner of the room. Mardone had just opened her mouth to speak when Winter's hand shot up.

Mardone sighed. "Yes, Miss Davenport?"

Winter's eyes darted around to make sure everyone was watching her. "Will we be covering special mental abilities in this class, Dean Mardone?"

Mardone's lips flattened into a straight line. "Were you paying attention during my introduction, Miss Davenport, or do you, too, struggle with being present?"

It was my turn to snicker. Winter scowled, but quickly smoothed it out. "Yes, of course, Dean Mardone. It's just that I hear a lot of noise, like static, but also voices—"

"The mediation techniques we cover in this class should help cut down on this *noise*, as you call it, but this is an entry-level course, suitable even for ursanthropes." She cast a patronizing look at Chad and the other bears. "Advanced mental abilities will be covered in-depth in a later course reserved for lycanthropes and ailuranthropes."

Winter's mouth twisted again, but this time I got the sense that she was actually upset. "But what should I do in the meantime?"

"Be quiet, Miss Davenport," Mardone sighed. "You should be quiet."

CHAPTER NINE

Crickets chirped and a gentle breeze rustled through the trees Thursday night as I made my way down the gravel path from the cafeteria behind Therian Hall to the domed building somehow officially known as The Shiftnasium—because that sounded *totally* official. I had decided to call it 'the gym' instead because my mouth refused to say such a ridiculous word.

Plus, that's all it was—a weight room, a cardio room, an indoor swimming pool, a basketball court, and a handful of classrooms. Pretty much the same as what they had to offer at Keller Parks. Nothing out of the ordinary at all.

My kind of place.

I knew all this because I had already been there earlier in the afternoon for Health & Physical Education for Shifters, the class that required the book *You, Your Body, and Your Other Body.* Dean Belhollow taught the health portion on Thursdays, and before class she had pulled me aside and given me a package of socks to replace the pair she'd swallowed.

It wasn't the sort of thing that would typically make me burst into tears—and I mean, she *did* owe me some socks—but the last three days had my normally resilient emotions worn a little raw, and there was just something so very *motherly* in the way she said, "Come here, honey, I got you a little something," that I somehow wound up snotting all over her burgundy blazer while she stroked my back and promised things would get better and I would come to love it here. I almost believed her.

My eyes had still been bloodshot when I walked into the classroom, so, of course, Winter took the opportunity to ask who I was getting my drugs from. That just made it all the more satisfying when Bellhollow walked in a moment later and, true to her word on my arrival, sent Winter outside to do twenty laps around the track under the blazing afternoon sun.

Winter had returned drenched, with runny mascara under her eyes and frizzy tendrils where her perfectly straight locks used to be. If before she had only wanted to destroy me socially, now she wanted to murder me. Literally. That's why, when I heard heavy footsteps crunching quickly down the path behind me that night, I clutched my book bag like a weapon and braced myself for an attempted assassination.

"Hey! Remi! Wait for us!" a guy's voice panted.

My death grip on my book bag relaxed. After three classes together, I knew the sound of that voice much too well, and even though Xander Danfield and I had yet to formally meet, I felt confident that he wouldn't make it out of the ring with a bunny rabbit, much less an emotionally frazzled, hyper-reactive werewolf girl like me.

I turned and waited for the figures bobbing in the darkness to catch up with me.

Great. Two nerds for the price of one.

I knew I shouldn't call them that—it felt very Winter-esque—but so far they had planted themselves in the front row of every single class, and, well, if the shoe fits...

"Hi, Xander. Kanze." I nodded to them each in turn.

Xander's eyes lit up, the way nerd eyes usually do when they find out you know their name. He pushed his thick-rimmed glasses up his nose and grinned. "Hi, Remi."

They were cute. I would give them that, even if their enthusiasm rubbed my relentless rationality the wrong way. Xander had light brown skin and wore his hair in short natural curls. His brown eyes gleamed with a warmth I'd found lacking in most of my peers here. Kanze was built with sharper angles and regarded me with apprehension from behind his mop of shaggy black hair.

"What's up, guys?" I asked, after several moments had passed with Xander just staring at me and Kanze just staring at him like he couldn't believe how bad he was blowing it.

"Um..." Xander fidgeted with the straps of his backpack. "Can we walk you to class?"

I didn't answer, just motioned toward the gym with my head and started walking again. Xander fell in right beside me while Kanze lagged a little behind.

"So, uh, how are you liking the Academy so far?" Xander asked.

I looked up to the sky and pretended to think for a moment. "Well, I've slept with a professor *and* a teaching assistant. Plus I smoked pot in Dean Belhollow's office... so I'd say I'm having a fantastic time. No complaints."

Xander's eyes widened and his Adam's apple jerked.

I nudged him with my elbow. "Not really. I haven't done any of those things."

"Oh, I know," he squeaked. "I didn't think—"

Kanze snickered in the background.

"And I don't make a habit of taking my clothes off in front of my classmates, so if that's why—"

"What? No!" Xander pulled on his backpack straps so the bulk of it hunched up over his shoulders like a turtle disappearing into its shell. "I didn't even see that."

"I did," Kanze piped up, and when I shot him a glare, he shrugged. "Just thought I'd be honest."

I let a little growl escape my throat, just for the fun of it. "How about *you* walk in front of us?" They seemed harmless enough, but I still didn't want either of them checking out my butt.

Kanze rolled his eyes, but took the lead as we continued down the path.

"Just ask her, dude," he muttered when several more seconds of awkward silence had passed. "We're almost there."

Xander took a deep breath. "Oh. Okay, well, Remi, the thing is, we were wondering, well, if you might, um..."

"Spit it out, Xander," I sighed.

He rubbed the back of his head and looked down at his shoes. "Would you maybe want to join our pack?"

I glanced from his hopeful face to Kanze's failed attempt to look nonchalantly over his shoulder. "Are you *both* asking me out?"

Kanze groaned and swung his head forward, shaking it. Xander's hands started working on his backpack straps again—his palms were so sweaty I could hear them squeaking on the vinyl.

"Because I'm not really looking for one boyfriend, much less two."

Laith's face flashed into my mind, but I quickly shook it out. *Absolutely not, Remi.*

"*What*? No way!" Xander said too fiercely. His backpack was all but on top of his head now. "This would definitely not be like that. Not at all. Nope. No way."

"I don't know, guys." We had reached the gym's

entrance. "I might just be more of a lone wolf."

Kanze leaned against the glass double doors, and I wondered if I had enough inner reserves of wolf strength to lift him out of my way. I just wanted to arrive at *one* class this week without any unfortunate incident. But the last thing my reputation needed was to get caught beating up on geeks. I could hear Winter now: *"It's not enough to steal all the boys, you have to take their lunch money too, James?"*

"Move," I growled.

"Just hear us out," Xander pleaded from beside me. "We think we'd make a really good team. We all have a strong commitment to reason and facts and the scientific process—"

I narrowed my eyes at him. "Who told you that?"

Fear flashed in Xander's eyes and he shrank back. "Who? Well, no one. We just—"

Kanze groaned at his friend's ineptitude. "Vice-Chancellor Gladwell. *She* told us to ask you. She said a pack has to have at least three members and 'be of mixed genders.'"

"Oh." My face burned hot. It's not like I wanted to be part of *anyone's* pack, but it still stung that even for the Gladwell AV Club I was just some kind of female-shaped quota they needed to fill. For the first time since this stupid dream started, I actually *wanted* to crawl out of my human skin.

"But we wanted to ask you anyway!" Xander glared at Kanze. "Right?"

"Yeah," Kanze deadpanned, wiggling his fingers in the air. "It'll be *super* fun."

Xander punched him on the arm. "You don't have to be such a—"

I stepped between them before Kanze could punch back. "Alright, alright, that's not going to help your case. If I have to join a pack, I guess I have to join a pack, but I'm not tying myself down with a couple of... goobers."

Kanze snorted. "See? I told you she was just like them."

This kid. I oughta...

"Just like who?" I demanded, going nose to nose with him.

Xander grabbed my elbow and tugged me back. I jerked out of his grasp, ready to swing my book bag at him after all.

He immediately lifted his hands, whether in surrender or to cover his face, I couldn't quite tell. "We wanted to ask you right away. I mean, *of course* we did, who wouldn't?"

I rolled my eyes. *Flattery will get you nowhere, bucko.*

Xander shrugged and looked down, and then he looked back up at me with an absolute killer pair of puppy dog eyes. "We just figured you probably wanted to join up with one of the cooler packs."

But guilt might.

Groaning, I pushed Kanze out of my way and yanked the door open, letting out a rush of frigid air conditioning. "Fine. Sure. I'll join your pack. I mean, why the hell not? What have I got to lose?"

Just a little thing called your dignity, *Remi.*

Xander yelped with either surprise or joy, but I wasn't waiting around to find out. I hurried down the hall, my footsteps echoing off the tile floor and concrete walls, obscuring the details of the whispered argument they were having back at the door.

A moment later, Xander caught up to me. If his tail had been on, it would have been wagging. "Did you mean it? You'll join our pack?"

"I don't say things I don't mean."

"Okay. Cool." He grinned. "Really cool. And hey, I'm sorry. I didn't want it to go like that."

"It's fine. It's not like it's a marriage proposal." I cut him a sideways look. "It's not a marriage proposal, right? I honestly have no idea how any of this works."

He shook his head. "It's just for class, I think. Group work, you know?"

I nodded. "Okay then." *All this drama over group projects?*

Kanze slunk up behind us, and Xander reached back to grab him and drag him forward. "Kanze is very happy too. He's just shy."

Kanze bared his teeth in a sarcastic, exaggerated smile that summed up pretty much all of my own feelings about being here. Then his face dropped back into deadpan. "We all do our own homework."

"You can count on it." I thrust out my hand and we shook on it.

"So what should our wolf names be?" Xander beamed back and forth between us. "I was thinking maybe we could do a space theme? I'll be Skywa—"

I clamped my hand over his mouth. "Dude. Don't make me regret this."

CHAPTER TEN

Shiftnasium Room A, where Health took place, had been an average, boxy classroom that smelled of disinfectant and shoes. Shiftnasium Room C turned out to be an entirely different story. When my new pack walked through the door, we found ourselves in an empty room with an elevator. A small sign invited us to push the single button. This caused a small scuffle between the boys, which Kanze won by yanking on Xander's backpack and letting its weight do the rest. After I helped Xander back onto his feet, we boarded the elevator for what seemed like a strangely long ride.

"It smells like wet dog," Xander complained,

pinching his nose.

The doors opened and the feeling of normalcy that the gym had given me vanished into thin air. We stepped out into a cavern, each of our mouths hanging ajar. Bright stadium lights hung from the rocky ceiling, illuminating an enormous, sawdust laden arena lined with rickety bleachers on either side.

"Um, I didn't order a rodeo," Kanze said. "Did you order a rodeo?"

"I can assure you I did *not* order a rodeo," Xander answered.

The rest of our class had already assembled in the center of the ring, and for reasons I could not fathom, they all appeared to be wearing loose-fitting paper underwear.

What fresh hell is this?

A hulking figure stepped in front of us, eclipsing the stadium lights. The man was probably in his early forties and had to be at least six-foot-seven. He wore a burgundy track suit instead of the standard faculty blazer, and every last inch of him bulged with muscles, even his neck. Sweat glistened on the dark skin of his bald head, and since it wasn't anywhere close to warm down here, I assumed this meant he was already angry.

"Nice of you mutts to show up," he snarled, raining tiny drops of spittle onto our faces.

Yep. Definitely angry.

I resisted the urge to wipe my face, but Kanze and Xander must have had death wishes. The dude—Dean Embry, I presumed— suddenly loomed even taller.

"Oh, I'm sorry. Did I mess up you pretty boys' make up?" His voice boomed loud enough to elicit several snickers from the students in the arena. Xander cringed, but Kanze's lip curled.

I side-stepped in front of them, pasting on a perky smile. "Where do we get our, um, our outfits, sir?"

Embry blinked once, like he couldn't believe I'd gotten between him and the nerds, and then screamed into my face, "Locker room! Now! Leave your shoes there, too!"

We followed his pointing finger to two doors set into the side of the cavern wall, one marked with a male stick figure, the other female. Inside, I found a stack of the paper undergarments next to the door. I reluctantly sat my book bag on one of the benches and removed my clothing, carefully tucking each item into the bag as I went, even my sneakers. I made a mental note to beat Winter back here after class because I had no doubt she'd steal my things and then accuse me of just *wanting* to be naked all the time.

I slipped into the paper boxer shorts and then tugged the paper bra over my head. A band of elastic at the hem held each of the garments in place around my ribs and hips, leaving my midriff uncomfortably bare, not to mention drafty.

Is this really necessary?

Stepping back out into the cavern, I found Xander and Kanze shirtless in their own paper boxers. Xander tried to hide his soft midsection behind his folded arms, but Kanze actually had a hint of a six-pack on his slender frame.

"Swim team, not karate," he said, catching me looking. "Before you ask."

I lifted my hands. "Wasn't going to."

We made our way out to the center of the arena, sawdust sifting between our toes.

Winter took one look at me and the shirtless nerds and laughed. "What is it with you and all these boys, James? Some kind of reverse harem fetish?"

I stepped closer, and noticed with no small amount of pride that I actually had a good two inches on her. "No, but since you brought it up, why do you think your boy Derek only invites girls into his pack?"

I glanced at her three minions, who were standing much closer to him than to her.

"Sexist much?" Winter scoffed. "This is *my* pack, not his."

"Sure." I lowered my voice. "But do *they* know that?"

She shoved me, *hard*, and I would have landed flat on my butt had Xander not caught me and set me upright again.

"What the hell is this?" Dean Embry bellowed.

Winter immediately squeezed her shoulders together so her boobs strained against her paper bra. She batted her eyelashes and spoke with a babyish pout. "I'm sorry, Dean Embry. It's just that she called you an ugly bear, and I don't put up with that kind of disrespect."

I gasped. "You—"

Embry glowered down at me. "That true?"

"No!" Xander said, stepping in front of me. "She's lying. Remi didn't say anything about you."

"Don't you raise your voice at me, son." He shook his head. "Damn wolves. You think you own this place." He pointed at Winter. "That goes for *you*, too." Embry moved away from me, leveling his eyes at every member of the class in turn. "But wolves don't own this classroom. I do. You best all remember that."

He walked farther out into the arena and turned to face us, crossing his arms over his massive chest. "My name is Gareth Embry, and I am the Dean of Physical Education. You will call me Dean Embry, Sir, at all times. You will not, under any circumstances, call me the *Gary the Were Bear* if you enjoy having all of your blood inside your body. Understand?"

Several of the jock types knew to shout, "Yes, sir, Dean Embry, sir!"

Embry nodded his approval at them, and then glowered at the rest of us, who had clearly never participated in organized sports or the army. "This class is Practical Shifting. It is what it sounds like it is. We're going to practice shifting. By the end of this semester, you should be able to shift on command, hold that shift for the duration of the class, and unshift on command. If you can't do that, you fail. Understand?"

This time, we *all* shouted, "Yes, sir, Dean Embry, sir!" and earned his approving nod.

Kanze raised his hand. "What happens if we fail?"

Embry stared at him blankly.

Kanze sighed. "What happens if we fail, Dean Embry, sir?"

Embry sidled over, scowling. "You planning to fail, pretty boy?"

"No," Kanze gritted out. "I'm just curious."

Embry laughed. "Are you a cat? You know what they say curiosity does to cats."

Kanze's fists clenched at his sides. "I'm a wolf, sir. But I still like to know things."

Embry chuckled again. "Well, know this! If you fail..." His eyes swept the class, silencing everyone who had laughed with him, and then he thundered, "I eat you for Christmas dinner!"

He whirled around and stomped several yards away, pausing with his back to us.

"This is the only class in which you will be allowed to wear those stupid paper panties," Embry said, unzipping his track jacket. "Your animal is naked, and feels no shame. Neither should you."

His jacket dropped to the sawdust, revealing the muscles that rippled all the way from his broad shoulders to his lean waist.

"Academy rules prohibit any of you from removing the paper panties at any time during Practical Shifting I. Should they be destroyed during your shift, your classmates will turn their backs while you unshift, and I will provide you with a new pair of paper panties." He gestured to a plastic sack on the ground near us. "However, since I graduated twenty years ago, these rules do not apply to me."

And with that, Dean Embry dropped his pants—and yes, somehow even his glutes looked like they would just as soon as kill us as teach us. One of Winter's minions emitted a throaty sound of appreciation that earned her a backslap on the arm from Winter, probably because it would be a lot harder to harass me about Professor Helms if one of her own was hot for teacher.

"I will now demonstrate a controlled shift and unshift," Embry continued, keeping his back to us. "Please do not panic. My prey instincts might be stimulated."

"Was that a joke?" Xander whispered. "Please tell me that was a joke."

"I don't think so," Kanze said, taking a step back.

An anxious hush fell over the crowd as Dean Embry moved his arms through a series of yoga-like poses, similar to what Laith had been doing in the promo video. But instead of running, Embry simply leaned forward and thick brown hair exploded from his back as he doubled—no, *tripled*—in size.

Wake up, wake up, wake up.

The Grizzly bear turned with surprising grace, his massive, clawed paws held in a muscle-man pose in front of his shaggy chest. He swung his enormous head from side to side, pinning each of us in turn with his beady brown eyes. Then he opened his jaws, revealing dripping yellow fangs, and roared. The force of the air leaving his lungs fluttered his jowls and a rancid mist settled over my skin.

Someone nearby gagged.

No, seriously, Remi. Wake up now.

The bear turned, dropping onto all fours, giving us a brief glimpse of his funny bobbed tail before the hair receded like a tide going back to the ocean. The hulking form shrank back to human proportions, which seemed hilariously flimsy now.

As Dean Embry pulled his pants back on, I suddenly became aware of sweaty fingers entwined with mine. I looked down at Xander's hand, and he quickly dropped it, folding both arms across his chest.

At least he didn't pee his paper.

Embry faced us, zipping up his jacket. He grinned, and I could not wrap my head around how his human teeth could be so white and clean when the bear's had been in such serious need of a dentist. Not that I could actually wrap my head around how this human had just been a bear either.

He slapped his hands together. "Who's up next?"

Winter, Chad, and Derek all shot their hands up. *Fine by me.* Earlier during dinner with Victoria—sans Laith—she had listened to my latest Winter horror story and explained that those three had been the first freshman to arrive this summer, way back in June. That had given them way too much time to forge their unholy alliance and get ahead of the game at shifting.

Embry pointed at Chad. "Bears first."

Chad pumped his fist and ran to the spot where Dean Embry had shifted. "Here?"

Embry nodded. "Do your thing."

Wait, that's it? No instructions?

Chad grinned and flexed his chest and biceps. He didn't bother with turning around or doing any of the stretches. He just closed his eyes and made a constipated face, and black hair erupted in uneven patches all over his body. He bore down even harder, bending his knees, and his body began to bulge and bend in ways that made me cringe.

Is that the sound of his bones *crunching?*

But the worst part was his face, the way his nose fused with his upper lip as jaw extended, the way his ears moved to the top of his flattening head, and his eyes—my stomach heaved as they shrank beneath his widening brow. When it was over, a large black bear stood before us with a few shreds of paper boxers still clinging to his fur. He awkwardly flailed his bear arms and made some strange huffing noises.

"Alright, everybody give it up for Chad!" Embry clapped. "You can un—"

But before he'd gotten the words out, the black bear convulsed, tumbling onto all fours, and a moment later, Chad was hunched naked on the ground. The class howled with laughter, and even though I wanted to, I bit my cheeks to keep it inside. I didn't want to legitimize the way they'd treated me.

Even if he does deserve it.

"Shut up!" Embry boomed. "Turn your backs!"

And that's pretty much how it went for the next hour, watching someone turn into a bear, shred their paper garments, and then turning around while Embry gave the naked humans a new pair.

"Is that all my bears?" Embry finally asked. "Wolves, you're up. Who's first?"

Kanze and Xander raised their hands, but without even being asked, Winter sashayed past Embry to the spot where the sawdust had been worn thin by all the bear paws. The nerds groaned and dropped their arms.

Winter turned her back and went through a series of arm movements that seemed like imitations of what I'd seen Laith and Embry do, not the real thing—whatever that was. She leaned her body to the right, letting her left hip pop past the hem of her paper short, and then repeated the action to the left until her shorts slipped enough that we could all see the tiny wolf paw print tattooed just above her butt.

Derek wolf whistled, and I swear I heard Xander and Kanze gulp loudly.

For the love of—

"None of that!" Embry shouted. "Next person to comment on another student's body spends this Saturday brushing my bear teeth." He pointed at Winter. "And you. Stop with the belly dance and shift already."

Winter vanished in a flash of white fur, but not before her skin flushed bright red.

The wolf faced us, tall and willowy. Her piercing blue eyes locked on me, and if I'd expected her wolf to somehow possess more humanity than her human, I knew in an instant I'd been wrong. Her lips curled, revealing strikingly white fangs.

I might have been terrified had the wolf not still

been wearing the paper bra and shorts. A snicker rippled through the class, and this time I let myself join in.

"Cut it out!" Embry barked. "You'll all be up there soon! Winter, unshift."

It happened instantly. She stood up with a smug smile, her underwear intact, and waltzed back over to the group, purposefully bumping into me. "Beat that, James."

Derek went next—a gray wolf—followed by the minions—two gray, one black. There were two other packs, full of students I recognized from class but had never interacted with. Standing next to the fidgety nerds, I wondered if I had sold myself short by accepting their offer so quickly.

Every time Embry asked, "Who's next?" I kept my arms clamped firmly to my sides. I had no idea how these people were doing what they were doing, and pride wouldn't let me give the nerds the satisfaction of mansplaining it to me. Meanwhile, Embry seemed intent on not giving the nerds the satisfaction of taking their turns, even though their hands shot up first every time.

But finally, it was just the three of us left.

Embry pointed at me. "Ladies first."

My head spun just thinking about getting stuck in that itchy fur coat again.

I took a step back. "Oh, that's okay. Let one of these guys go first."

"Oh, come on, Remi," Winter chirped fake-sweetly. "You're such a pro! Longest freshman shift in Gladwell history!"

Embry rubbed his chin. "That's right. I should have let a superstar like you go first."

"What?" I squeaked. "No. That was an accident. I didn't know how to... to get *out*."

Embry laughed. "Nah, don't be modest. Come on up here. Show these amateurs how it works."

Sweat broke out under my arms and I clamped them to my sides so no one would see it dripping. I shook my head. "No, really, I don't know how."

"Oh, come on, Remi!" Winter pleaded, an evil smile curling the edges of her mouth. "Show us what you've got!"

Chad put his fingers in his mouth and whistled while Derek clapped. "Show us what you've got!"

A wave of peer pressure swept the class, and within seconds, everyone except Xander and Kanze was chanting, "*Show us what you've got!*"

"You hear the crowd, Remi. Come on up!" Embry

kicked an X into the sawdust. "Right here."

I looked to Xander and Kanze for help, but they were scowling because he wasn't letting them have their turn. *Great pack solidarity, guys.*

"St. James," Embry growled. "*Now*, please. Don't make me ask again."

Taking a deep breath like the Chancellor taught me, I squared my shoulders and strode over to the X. Embry moved back several feet, smiling broadly as the chanting faded to silence.

"Now shift."

I stood there. Feeling like I might as well have been naked as wearing these stupid paper clothes.

"Well, go on," Embry said in a falsely encouraging tone.

I tried to summon my wolf by remembering the way I'd felt yesterday in meditation class when I'd wanted to let it out to tear Winter limb from limb.

But again, nothing happened.

It was like my wolf had gone into hiding.

"St. James, you seem to be under the impression we have all night," Embry said. "But you are wrong. So *shift*."

Wrapping my arms around myself, I said in a small voice, "I don't know how."

"She doesn't know how!" Embry hollered. "She says she doesn't know how."

The class snickered. Someone applauded.

"You can do it, Remi!" Winter shouted, and I wished she'd go back to calling me James. "You're a legend!"

"Come on, Remi!" Xander cheered, and threw in a whoop for good measure.

"I can't," I whispered to Embry. "I really don't know how. It's only ever just happened to me."

"I see, I see," Embry said softly and came closer again, putting himself between me and the class. He bent his head toward mine and spoke in a low murmur. "Maybe you don't understand what's going on here. You *will* shift, St. James. So you'd better figure it out quick."

CHAPTER ELEVEN

"Six weeks." Chancellor Gladwell closed the manila folder and drummed his fingers on top of it. He scrunched up his face and looked to his wife, seated on his right hand at the far end of the glossy mahogany conference table. "Has it really been six weeks?"

"Yes, Oberon." Vice-Chancellor Gladwell placed her hand over his to quiet his fidgeting. "The question is, why?" She cast her eyes to my end of the table. "And what now?"

Dean Belhollow squeezed my elbow. She was the only professor sitting near me. Dean Embry sat at the Chancellor's left hand, next to Professor Helms, who sat across from Dean Mardone, who sat beside the

Vice-Chancellor. We were in the Board Room behind the Chancellor's offices in the top of Therian Hall's spired tower, and the floor-to-ceiling window behind them showed the formerly blue-green mountains blazing red, orange, and gold beneath a blanket of smoky gray fog.

I pulled my arms off the table, leaving two sweaty hand prints where my palms had been pressed. I tried to dry them discreetly on the simple black skirt Belhollow had advised me to wear to this emergency progress review. Six pairs of eyes studied my every move.

But that's nothing new.

No one had seen hide nor hair of Wolf Remi in six weeks. Not since that first day when she'd tried to take a bite out of Winter Davenport and suddenly turned back into naked, human me—an incident Winter still reminded me of daily, as though a loser of my magnitude could ever pose any threat to her undisputed Class Alpha status.

"Six weeks," the Chancellor repeated, running a hand through his floppy gray hair. "This is highly unusual."

Dean Mardone snorted and tossed her red mane. "Unusual? Chancellor, it's completely *unheard* of, and you damn well know that. It's high time we—"

The Vice-Chancellor held up a hand, almost directly in front of Mardone's face. "Get to the bottom of this, yes. Does anybody have any *constructive* thoughts on the subject?"

Dean Embry leaned forward, folding his massive forearms on the table. "I can solve this mystery for you right now, Vice-Chancellor. This girl is stubborn as a mule. That's it. That's all this is." He leaned back in his plush boardroom chair again, shaking his head and glaring in my direction. "She's a shifter. She can shift. She just *won't*."

Mardone pursed her bright red lips. "I disagree."

Embry lifted his eyebrows. "Seriously, Lenore?"

"Oh, she's stubborn, no doubt about that. She won't even pretend to take my class seriously." Mardone rolled her eyes, which I have to admit *is* pretty much all I could do during the ninety minutes we spent together each Monday and Wednesday. "But no one—and certainly no one her age—could intentionally hold back a shift for six weeks. We all know this, even if some of us don't want to admit it. You lock a dog in a room, it's going to chew its way out."

"Watch your language," the Vice-Chancellor

growled.

Mardone laughed. "Oh, please, Cordelia. I'm one of *three* ailuranthropes on the entire campus. Don't pretend my obvious use of metaphor was oppressing you."

The Chancellor cleared his throat. "Let's stay on topic, ladies. What are you saying, Lenore? If she's not refusing, then she's what, a—"

"A dud?" Mardone threw up her hands. "Yes! Clearly!"

Both Gladwells sighed, and Belhollow's chair squeaked like she might be preparing to go over the table.

The Chancellor held an apologetic hand out toward me. "Remi, that is not the word I was going to use."

"There is no such thing as a dud at the Gladwell Academy," the Vice-Chancellor said firmly.

I shrugged, feeling very small in my overstuffed, high-backed chair. "Maybe I'm the first."

Mardone smiled triumphantly, while Embry snorted with contempt. Professor Helms chewed on his lower lip and traced the grain of the table with one thumbnail.

"What makes you say that, Remi?" the Vice-

Chancellor asked. "Care to shed some light on your experience of this dilemma?"

My eyes darted to Belhollow, who offered an encouraging smile. We had grown close these past six weeks, or at least it felt that way to me. Her portion of Health & Physical Education for Shifters was the only class that contained anything approximating facts, and I often found myself gravitating to her office in the health clinic throughout the week, examining the human and animal anatomy charts on the walls while she sang the praises of the Health and Science Major.

I still had some faint hope of waking up from this nightmare before I had to choose a career path, but since the only other majors offered were Physical Education with Dean Embry and Liberal Arts with Dean Mardone, I had grudgingly begun to imagine a future in shifter healthcare.

Not if you don't get your wolf back.

"Sometimes..." I started, and then swallowed the lump in my throat. "Sometimes I get this prickly sensation, like up and down my arms, or on my back, and I think, 'Oh, no, it's happening!' and it's like a wall comes down. Nothing happens after all."

Professor Helms drew in a sharp breath, but no one else noticed because Embry pounded his fist on the table and shouted, "Aha! See! Right there. She thinks 'oh no' and then she shuts it down. Who does that? Who thinks 'oh no' when they start to shift?"

"Maybe someone who had a traumatic experience her first day on campus?" Belhollow countered, and even though I knew she was on my side, my face flushed red. I didn't want the faculty thinking about me naked on the floor in the Great Hall. She sighed and continued. "I've done a thorough physical examination and found nothing that would be preventing her shifts. I believe Remi is suffering from a mental block. *Unintentionally.*" She glared at Embry.

The Gladwells glanced at each other. The Chancellor shrugged, and the Vice-Chancellor turned her eyes back to me. "Remi, when was the last time you felt like you might *actually* shift?"

My mind travelled through back time. I felt the prickling often, but the last time anything had come of it had been that day in the bookstore. My lips parted to say so, but Professor Helms caught my eye as though he could read my mind. His head shook almost imperceptibly.

"Um..." I trailed off.

Dean Mardone blew air through her lips. "Oh, I can tell you that. Every day in my class."

"Those are just prickles." I ducked my head to hide the blush. "And how would you even know that?"

She shot me a withering glare, leaning in my direction. "Because unlike you, I take my meditation practice seriously, and I am in tune to my surroundings in ways you can't even imagine. I can *feel* every time you prickle." She spat out the last word.

The Chancellor frowned. "Well, Lenore, that seems like relevant information you might have shared with us sooner."

Mardone turned to him with a syrupy smile. "I didn't want to embarrass the child, Oberon, considering what triggers these episodes."

My skin prickled now, but with rage, not the stirrings of the wolf. My hands clenched around the arms of my chair, and Belhollow reached over and grabbed my wrist, as if to remind me that my manners needed to be minded, even if no one else's were.

"Lenore, please explain." The Vice-Chancellor rubbed her temple like she needed more coffee—or something even stronger.

Me too, V.C., me too.

Mardone shrugged and her breasts nearly heaved

out of her blazer, making Professor Helms' eyes widen across the table. He quickly lowered his head and seemed to dig his thumbnail even deeper into the table.

"Whenever my teaching assistant so much as breathes in her vicinity, Remi gets, shall we say, shifty."

That's not true!

I bit down on the inside of my cheek to keep from saying anything out loud. It was only *partially* not true. Laith Brighton did still bring out the beast in me, but he had to do a little more than breathe. He had to bite one side of his lip while the other side smiled after we exchanged barbs, or he had to come up behind me and correct my slumping shoulders as I sat dozing on my meditation mat.

"And who is your teaching assistant?" the Chancellor asked.

"Laith Brighton." Mardone purred his name like she owned him, and the hackles on my neck rose, wolf or no wolf.

"Oh," Belhollow said softly beside me, and a moment later the Chancellor very loudly echoed, "Ohhhhh!"

He glanced at his wife, who peered at me with

furrowed brows. She tapped her finger on the side of her head. "I wonder..."

"If I may speak!" Professor Helms said way too loudly, making everyone in the room jump. He immediately shrank back in his chair.

The Chancellor made a dramatic show of putting a finger in his ear. "Go ahead, Dan. Don't be shy or anything."

Helms cleared his throat. His smile wavered, and a cluster of butterflies made a lap around my stomach. I had been carefully cultivating a crush on him all semester to distract myself from Laith. It's not like I thought anything was going to come of it, but whenever my thoughts drifted to Laith and his stupid eyes and his stupid smile and his stupid forearms and his stupid neck, I would just gently bring my thoughts back to Professor Helms and his adorable, absent-minded professor aesthetic.

And Mardone says I haven't learned anything from meditation!

"Right, then." Helms flattened his palms on the table and took a deep breath. "Well, as I've sat here listening, it's occurred to me that perhaps what Miss St. James requires is some one-on-one attention. It's not been so long since I was a student myself—" He laughed nervously, like he didn't really want to bring that up. "—and Practical Shifting can be quite an overwhelming class. The paper vests. Everyone staring."

Embry scoffed. "Everybody wears the same stupid paper underpants and gets stared at by the same eyes, but nobody else is having problems. Even those nerds she packed up with are holding shifts for up to ninety minutes now."

Oof. Low blow, dude.

"My class is not the problem." Embry pointed at me. "*She* is the problem."

"On that, we can agree," Mardone said. "But what can we do? We can't even—"

The Vice-Chancellor slammed her hand on the table. "Mind your tongue, Dean."

Mardone scowled. "I'll mind it, but you still know what I mean."

Embry frowned, glancing between the women suspiciously. "I'm not sure I—"

"Let me work with her privately," Belhollow cut in, resting her hand on my shoulder. "Daniel may be on to something."

The Vice-Chancellor sighed. "I think it's as good an idea as any."

Embry laughed. "If I can't teach her to shift, no one can."

"You don't teach!" I blurted out, banging my fists on the arms of my chair.

Six pair of eyes widened at me. Embry's lip curled back in a sneer. "Come again?"

My instincts told me to sink into my chair, maybe expose my throat like a chastened puppy, but my commitment to the truth overpowered them.

"You don't teach," I repeated in as steady a voice as I could muster. "You've never taken one second to tell us *how* to shift or unshift. It's just, do this, do that, figure it out right now."

Embry's jaw flexed. "You might have a point if you weren't the only student on the verge of flunking out their first semester."

Flunking out? No one had used that kind of language yet. Panic bubbled in my lungs, making it hard to breathe. It's not like I'd ever wanted to be at this stupid Academy, but too much time has passed to return to the life I'd been planning. My scholarship to Keller Parks was long gone. I had no money, no car to drive home in.

No home to drive to.

"Even Robert Borden made it to his second

semester," Mardone said, like this would really explain what a screw-up I was.

"Who's Robert Borden?" My voice came out way too high. "What happens if I flunk out?"

"No one's flunking out." The Vice-Chancellor glared at Mardone. "And don't you worry about Robert Borden. Entirely different story. As long as you're willing to make an effort, you'll always have a place here."

Belhollow tucked a strand of hair behind my ear. "We aren't going to kick you out for something you can't help, sweetie. You and I will work together, and we'll get your wolf back." She smiled, and if we'd been alone, I might have fallen onto her shoulder and cried like the day she gave me the socks.

"Ah, if I might speak again?" Helms said, at a normal volume this time.

The Chancellor threw his hands up in the air. "For the love of shifting, Dan! You're in America now. You don't have to be so polite all the time. If you've got something to say, just jump on in."

"Oh. Alright. Yes." Helms bit his lip, but then he couldn't hold it back. "Sir."

The Chancellor slumped forward, propping one elbow on the table and resting the side of his face in that hand. "I'm hungry, Daniel. Come on."

Daniel—I mean, Professor Helms—swallowed hard and shifted in his chair. "Well, it's just that what I meant to say earlier, what I wished to suggest... Perhaps Remi might benefit more from instruction by someone of her... own kind?"

My own kind. Normally, I hated when professors talked like that—which they did *all* the time—but something about the way he said it made my heart flutter against my ribs.

Belhollow chuckled. "Surely you aren't suggesting yourself, Daniel?"

He shrugged and looked down at his lap. "Well, I just mean to say that I'm willing. That's all. If the Gladwells felt it might be in her best interest."

"I hardly think that would be appropr—" Belhollow started.

The Chancellor cut her off. "We're all adults here, Cherish. Even Remi. No need to molly-coddle her. Not with a guy like Dan." He waved his hand at Helms dismissively and Helms' jaw tightened. "I say let him give it a shot. Cordelia?"

The Vice Chancellor looked from me to Helms and back again. "I think Daniel has a point, Cherish. No offense to you, of course. But we'll leave it up to Remi.

Would you be comfortable taking private lessons from Professor Helms?"

Belhollow shot me a look that said, *You can say no.*

But Helms was also shooting me a look from beneath his thick eyelashes. A look both shy and pleading, and even though I didn't want to hurt Belhollow's feelings by not working with her, I also kind of really didn't want to say no.

CHAPTER TWELVE

"I've got it." Xander dropped his dinner tray on our usual table in the corner of the food court. He grinned as he plopped down next to Kanze. "Cerberus."

I gave him a look over the panini I hadn't quite gotten to my lips fast enough. "You know I don't speak geek."

"Do you mean Greek?" Xander waggled his eyebrows with a grin.

"I meant what I said." I stuffed the crispy edge of the panini into my mouth and closed my eyes, savoring the juicy roast beef. I'd always eaten meat in what I'd considered normal amounts, but lately it had become an obsession, which if left un-indulged would quickly transform into a frantic need.

When I opened my eyes, Kanze was shaking his head. "I don't think I like where this is going."

Xander groaned. "Come on, dude. It's *perfect*."

I raised my hand that wasn't clutching the panini. "Still have no idea what you're talking about."

Kanze rolled his eyes. "He wants us to dress up like a three-headed dog."

"Nope. Uh-huh. Not happening." I shook my head, ripping off another chunk of panini because I couldn't resist it anymore. "Not in a million years."

Xander threw his hands up. "Guys! It guards the gates of Hell!"

This time, I didn't bother swallowing before I said, "And that's where you're going soon if you don't shut up."

Xander banged his head on the table, nearly spilling his steaming bowl of stew. For a split second, I seriously considered snatching it off his plate and guzzling it down.

"Don't. Touch. It." he growled, curling his arm around it without lifting his head.

He's still sore about last time.

Kanze grabbed Xander's shoulder and tugged him upright. "I never even agreed to matching costumes, much less *sharing* one."

"And I never agreed to costumes at all." I shuddered. "Sorry, boys, but Halloween ain't really my thing."

Xander made a face like I'd punched him. "You're killing me, Remi. We are not letting you spend Halloween night moping in your room. I mean, it's *a Ball*. It's like Prom, but without all the mean kids."

"Are you kidding me right now?" I cut my eyes at the table where Winter's pack sat laughing it up, most likely at my expense.

Xander glanced over and shrugged. "She's not that bad. All she does is talk."

A scoff escaped me. "Easy for you—"

"Has she ever put you in a dumpster?" Kanze asked.

Xander lifted an eyebrow. "Or dunked your head in a toilet and stole your shoes while you were upside down gasping for air?"

I sighed and looked down at my plate. "No."

"See? All talk. Plus, she keeps those goons on a tight leash."

Kanze stroked his chin, gazing almost dreamily in her direction. "I think she's just very insecure."

Xander made a grunt of agreement. "Definitely. It's like, who hurt her, you know?"

I kicked them both in the shins, eliciting two high-pitched yelps.

"What's Pack Rule Number Two, guys?"

Kanze grimaced, rubbing his leg under the table. "No crushing on the enemy."

"And in light of this Ball, let's review Pack Rule Number One."

"No crushing on you," Xander mumbled, shoving a spoonful of stew into his mouth.

"Very good." I took another bite of panini, and this time it sent familiar prickles racing up and down my arms. "I will go to the stupid Ball, but I'm not wearing a costume, and I'm not going to dance."

"Well, damn." The chair beside me squealed out from the table, and my least favorite person dropped into it. "Here I'd been hoping you'd go as a sexy lion tamer." Laith made the sound and motion of cracking a whip.

The nerds' wide eyes bounced back and forth between us.

"Ugh." I turned slightly away from him, so I wouldn't have to see that stupid, lip-biting grin. Now I knew where those prickles really came from. "Never mind. I'm not going."

Laith reached over and stole a stray piece of roast beef off my plate. I swiped at his wrist, but he already had it in his mouth, chewing. He gave me a proud, tight-lipped smile. "You know, I heard a rumor about you, St. James."

Sighing, I stared resolutely at the grill marks on my panini as I brought it back to my mouth. Laith walked his fingers over to my plate and snatched a second piece. This time, my hand slammed down, flattening his to the table. My head turned toward him, growling, and suddenly our faces were very close. The prickles rolled down my back.

His smile grew. He jerked his hand out from under mine, and then rolled it over, revealing the meat still in his palm. He slapped it to his mouth and chewed slowly.

"Dude, get your own. It's not like it costs anything."

"Don't you want to know what I heard about you?"

I slammed my sandwich down, making the nerds jump. "What, Laith? It's not a secret that I can't shift. Are you here to tell me how I could if only I'd just sit still and go 'om, om, om' three times a day?"

His head snapped back, eyes darkening, but he maintained his grin. "No. I just wanted to know if it's true that you're pregnant with quadruplets and one of them is mine."

I buried my face in hands and stifled a scream.

"Wait, what? You're pregnant?" Xander squeaked, but it cut off funny at the end so I assumed Kanze elbowed him.

"No!" I dropped my hands, glaring at both nerds. "And this is why we don't—"

"Crush on the enemy," Kanze said again. "We get it."

Laith pushed his lips into a sad pout. "So no baby for us?"

My hands balled up into fists and I slammed them onto the table so I wouldn't use them on his stupid perfect face. "I'm just hungry, okay? I'm very stressed!"

His brows furrowed. "Hmm."

I waited, but he didn't continue. "Hmm what?"

"Maybe your wolf is stress eating. Because she's locked up." My face must have turned a murderous shade of red, because he threw his hands up in surrender. "Whoa, whoa, I'm just thinking out loud here."

Leaning in closer, I growled into his face. "Well, think *quieter*."

Our eyes held on each other for a moment longer than they ever had before. The prickling spread across my entire body, and it was all I could do not to stop, drop, and roll like my clothes were on fire. Finally, Laith ducked his head and broke the weird spell.

"Listen," he said softly. "There's a reason they put me in that stupid video. If you want any help with letting your wolf out—"

"From you?" I laughed. "No, thanks. I've already got a tutor."

He leaned away from me, and for a second there, I must have been losing my mind because I thought he actually looked hurt.

He cleared his throat. "Oh, yeah?"

"It's Professor Helms, if you must know," I blurted out, then tore off much too big a chunk of panini. *Way to play it cool, Remi.*

He made a choked sound. "Remi, that's not—"

"Perhaps your time would be better spent sharing your vast wisdom with your *girlfriend*." I pinned him with another glare. "Or, better yet, letting her share some with you. Like 'no one cares what you think, Laith.'"

His features blanked, like even his soul had checked out.

Probably some stupid meditation technique for nursing a wounded ego.

He scooted his chair back from the table and stood up very straight, his lean stomach just inches from my face. His scent slammed into my nose, and my brain broke it down into its respective parts at lightning speed—flannel, cotton, denim, leather, sweat, roast beef, citrus, and...*teakwood?*—and then rolled out an unbidden montage of kissing scenes. Him and me. Hands and hair and skin and—

"Why are you still standing there?" I snarled, digging my fingers into my panini. There were prickles all over my body that had *nothing* to do with shifting.

Laith snorted, and his breath fluttered the hair at my temple. "Y'all boys deserve medals for letting this one in your pack."

He walked away, and I slammed my panini down, dropping pieces of meat all over the plate. "Can you believe that guy?"

Xander and Kanze dropped their wide-eyed stares. Kanze busied himself with his pizza while Xander stared into his empty bowl and pushed his glasses up his nose.

"What?" I demanded.

They both shrugged.

"*What?*" I repeated, my voice deadly.

Kanze shook his black hair out of his eyes. "You were kind of mean, Remi."

I scoffed. "*I* was mean? Didn't you hear him?"

Xander twisted his mouth to one side and rubbed the back of his head. Kanze stuffed half his slice of pizza in his face.

I pushed my chair back and slung my book bag over my shoulder. "Well, excuse me for not being insecure enough to earn your sympathy."

They shared a knowing sideways glance that only deepened my fury. I swiped my tray off the table and considered which one I should backhand with it.

"Oh, and by the way, thanks for asking about my progress review. I'm so glad I had the chance to confide in my friends about the fact that if I don't shift soon, I'm going to fail."

Kanze perked up. "Fail? Did they say what happens if you fail?"

My jaw dropped. "*That's* your response?"

His brow furrowed. "I think it's a reasonable question, which *no one* here will answer for me. I just thought—"

"Dude, shut up." Xander scrambled to his feet. "Remi, wait."

But I was already walking—as fast as I could without running across the cafeteria like a crazy person. I brushed past Winter's table, which immediately made them all cackle as though my very existence were the funniest thing on Earth.

"You shouldn't be carrying that bag, James!" Winter called after me. "It's not good for the babies!"

***

The treadmill couldn't go fast enough. The step machine couldn't climb high enough. The rowing machine couldn't row anywhere, much less far enough away from this whole Gladwell Academy nightmare to make me feel like a real person again.

I turned to one of the punching bags, not bothering with the gloves we were supposed to use. My sweaty hair clung to my forehead and neck as I pummeled the red plastic until the skin on my knuckles cracked. I pulled my stinging fingers to my lips, sucking the thin lines of blood that trickled out.

I don't know, Remi, this feels pretty damn real.

It did. It felt like actual pain happening to my actual body.

And if I were honest with myself, so had every toe stub, paper cut, and post-run side stitch I'd felt in the past six weeks. So had every cruel word, epic fail, and unrequited rush of desire.

I'm not dreaming, am I?

With an anguished cry, I shoved the punching bag as hard as I could. It slammed into the wall, bounced back, and knocked me to the floor.

This is my life.

The truth swirled around my stunned head like little cartoon birds as I lay on the soft blue mat, catching my breath. I'm not sure how long I laid there before a familiar brown hand hovered into view.

"Okay, this is getting ridiculous," Victoria said. "Do I need to get you a walker?"

Groaning, I let her haul me to my feet. *My real feet.* My knees wobbled between the aching muscles of my thighs and calves, and she eased me onto a bench against the wall. *The real wall.* Victoria sat beside me, concern radiating from her eyes. *Her real eyes.*

A wave of guilt rolled over me. Victoria was a real person with real feelings for a real guy who I also had real feelings for. Yes, they were only real in the sense that they weren't just dream feelings like I'd been telling myself all semester, not real in the sense that they were anything more than a stupid crush, but still.

I'm a real bad friend.

"Are those tears?" Victoria leaned in closer, squinting at my face. "Those are tears. Are you hurt?"

I shook my head and wiped my eyes on my forearm. "I'm fine. Really. Just a bad day." A wry laugh escaped me. "Bad year."

"Hmm." Victoria tapped her index finger on her lips and then pointed it at me. "I know just what you need. Come on."

She grabbed my elbow and dragged me off the bench and out the door before I could even ask what was happening. The clock in the empty Shiftnasium hallway read six-thirty.

"Where are we going?" I pulled out of Victoria's grip because it was throwing me off balance. "I have a meeting with Professor Helms at eight."

Victoria frowned. "That seems late."

Ugh, not you, too.

"He's going to try to help me shift before Wolf Music at nine." I shoved my hands into the deep front pocket of my hoodie. "I've never been able to participate."

She side-eyed me. "And you're sad about that?"

I shrugged. "I have to sit there for three hours no matter what, and it would probably be a lot less terrifying if I weren't the only thing in the room looking like a snack."

Victoria shuddered. "Laith and I have to wear noise-cancelling headphones to block out the sound. I wish they'd do it off-campus. No offense."

"Is that why Laith hates wolves so much?" I asked, following Victoria into Shiftnasium Room C. "And why are we in here?"

"You'll see." Victoria pressed the elevator's down arrow button. "And the howl fest certainly doesn't help matters, but that's not why Laith... is so Laith."

The elevator doors opened and we stepped inside. As soon as the doors closed, the wet dog stench threatened to make me gag. I now knew it was the smell of thirty years' worth of sweaty shifters coming back from Practical Shifting classes.

"So why is Laith so *Laith*?" I asked, then shook my head. "I'm sorry. That's none of my business."

Victoria laughed and nudged me with her elbow. "Of course it's your business. He is the father of one of your babies after all."

The blood drained from my face. I could feel it sliding backwards down every vein in my neck. "That's not—I'm not—I've never—"

Victoria laughed harder, clutching my shoulder. "Remi, relax. It was a joke. Not funny yet?"

"Oh. Okay." I leaned against the stupidly slow elevator's wall, waiting for my heart to start pumping again. "Good. That's good. Ha."

She shook her head, still chuckling. "You looked like you thought I was taking you down here to murder you."

I smiled weakly. "It would be a murder-worthy offense."

"Oh, there'd be a murder, but it would be him, not you."

The elevator door opened, letting in a blast of cold cave air. I immediately shrank deeper into my hoodie.

Victoria slung her arm over my shoulders. "Sisters before misters, right?"

"Right," I squeaked, wishing I could shift into a mouse and dig a tiny hole to bury myself and all my stupid Laith-induced prickles in.

Victoria led me around to the right side of the arena and up the rickety bleachers. She balanced easily on the top row, but I had to keep one hand on the rough cavern wall to feel anywhere close to safe. As we walked, she softly counted off the number of stalactites we had to duck under. Finally, she paused under number seven.

"Here we are." She patted the jagged rock.

"Wow," I tried to sound suitably impressed. "That's a really cool one."

Victoria's laugh echoed eerily through the cave. "Don't worry. I didn't bring you down here to see a rock that looks exactly like every other rock."

And then she jumped and disappeared into the ceiling.

I'm not sure what I thought was happening, but I screamed and slammed my back against the cavern wall. More eerie laughter echoed above my head. Looking up, I found Victoria's hand reaching down to me once again—at least I was still on my feet.

It took a moment for my eyes to adjust to the darkness behind her. She was perched on a ledge hidden by the stalactite, a wide grin across her face. "What are you waiting for?"

I stared warily at her hand. She'd never steered me wrong before, but I couldn't see what good could possibly come from going up there—or how I'd ever get back down without tumbling down the bleachers.

And there was that meeting with Professor Helms scratching at the back of my mind. If I squinted just right, he might even be cuter than that obnoxious mountain lion.

"Remi, come on," Victoria said, her voice firmer now. "Trust me. I'll pull you up."

Squeezing my eyes shut so I couldn't see all my bones breaking, I grasped Victoria's hand. With one solid tug, she lifted me off my feet, and a moment later I was sprawled on the ledge, only my feet dangling over the edge.

"When Laith and I do this, whoever follows bites the other one's tail—"

Whoa, wait, what *are we doing?*

CHAPTER THIRTEEN

"You should have told me you were claustrophobic," Victoria said as she helped me squeeze out of the narrow tunnel we'd spent the last fifteen minutes in.

I collapsed onto my stomach, sucking in the sweet fresh forest air. "I didn't know."

"I guess this wasn't such a good surprise then." She chuckled. "Surprise! You've got a debilitating fear!"

"I mean, better to find out now than after I flunk out and have to become a coal miner." I rolled over on my back and gasped at the number of stars lighting up the night.

"A coal miner?" Victoria leaned back against of the boulders shielding the opening to her secret tunnel.

"Isn't that what people do around here?" I asked, moss crunching under my palms as I sat up.

"Maybe? I don't know." She shrugged. "I'm from Texas."

"Do you miss it?"

She smiled and her eyes wandered off across the sky. "I miss the food. My family sometimes. But mostly the food."

I scooted around so we were facing the same direction. We were perched on a rocky outcropping in the middle of a gently sloping forest. A chilly breeze whistled through the leaves and several let go and drifted to the ground.

"This is really nice," I said, gesturing at the woods and the stars. "I didn't realize how trapped I was starting to feel inside that damn wall."

"It's rough," she agreed. "But next semester, your pack will be assigned a perimeter patrol. That can be fun."

I picked at a tuft of dried grass poking from a crack in the boulder. "If there *is* a next semester."

"Remi—"

"Do you know anything about Robert Borden?" I cut her off before she could lie to me about how everything was going to turn out fine. "Mardone said he flunked out."

Victoria made a face. "That was a very different situation."

"What happened to him?" I pressed.

She sighed, like she really didn't want to talk about it. "He went... feral."

I scrunched my brow. "What does that mean?"

"It means..." She chewed on her lip, searching for words. "His wolf mind was stronger than his human mind. Even when he was a person."

My eyes went wide. "That can happen?"

"It's very, *very* rare," Victoria said quickly. "And Robert was very, very troubled. As a person. He was always looking for fights. It wasn't safe to have him here."

"What did they do with him?" My mind raced with possibilities, none of them good. "I mean, they couldn't just let him go..."

Can they even let me go?

Victoria shrugged. "I guess he went to the pound." My eyes must have popped out of my head because she quickly said, "Shifter jail. Laith calls it the pound."

I gulped. "There's a *shifter jail?*"

"Well, yeah. I mean, okay, we don't know for *sure* that it exists, but there has to be something like that, right? Not all shifters are going to be nice people."

A dark laugh escaped me. "Can you nominate people for shifter jail? I've got a few candidates..."

She playfully bumped my shoulder. "Is my boyfriend on that list?"

I groaned and buried my face in my hands. "I'm sorry. I don't know why we want to kill each other."

She laughed. "Cats and dogs. It's a powerful thing."

"But I don't want to kill you."

"Uh, because I'm awesome!" She laughed, but then grew serious. "But Laith doesn't want to kill you, Remi. He's actually... he's really worried about you. This meeting with Helms..."

My body went stiff. "Is my only chance at staying out of the pound."

"That's not true." Victoria turned toward me, reaching for my arm, but I pulled it away. She dropped her hand. "Laith said he offered—"

My head snapped around. "Did he put you up to this? Did he tell you to talk to me?"

She shook her head, but the truth was plain on her face.

"Ugh!" I started to get up. "He needs to mind his own business. He can't talk to me like—"

"Whoa, slow down." Victoria caught my arm and pulled me back down. "This moss is slick. You could slide right off."

I settled back onto the rock, but my body was prickling—the way it only seemed to prickle when Laith was around. The trouble was that as much as I genuinely did want him to mind his own business, the fact that he wasn't... well, that made me feel all kinds of warm and gooey inside. And the last thing I needed right now was for Victoria to realize her boyfriend made me feel like a half-baked chocolate chip cookie.

"So how did you two get together?" I blurted, my voice a little too high and tight.

"What? Oh, well, you know. Only two cats on campus." Her voice also jumped an octave. "Fate, I guess."

Fate? That was not something I believed in, but if Victoria believed in it, that must mean her feelings for Laith weren't just any old feelings. They were love.

My heart sank, which made zero sense. Of all the parts of my body that responded positively to Laith Brighton, my heart wasn't really one of them. I at least had that much under control. Did I sometimes imagine pushing him up against the wall in Dean Mardone's candlelit classroom and tangling my fingers in his hair and—okay, yeah, sure. Guilty as charged. But did I imagine us going on dates, hold hands, watching sappy movies? No. Of course not. My feelings for Laith were pure animal lust.

So why do I feel so sad?

"So it's pretty serious then?" I asked, hoping I sounded truly interested and not, you know, *interested.*

Victoria smiled just as a cloud covered the moon, and the sudden darkness made her smile seem nervous, not coy like I knew it must be. "I think... I think it might be going somewhere."

"That's great." I made myself smile, but it felt too big and too false, so I quickly added, "If you've acquired that taste."

She laughed lightly and tucked her dark hair behind her ear. "I sure have."

We fell quiet for a moment, watching the wispy clouds float across the starry sky. I hugged myself against the chill creeping into my hoodie.

"I understand if you don't want to let Laith help you," Victoria said after a while, breaking the silence. "And I know you two will probably always rub each other wrong."

I cringed at the unbidden image of Laith rubbing me right.

"But Laith had a bad first year too," Victoria continued, oblivious to my internal struggle. "Being the only lion in his class was like having a target on his back. I mean, my first year wasn't great either, but it's different for girls. Name-calling and stupid rumors." She shot me a knowing smile, but it didn't last. "But for guys, it's like, anything goes, you know? The wolves that year made his life hell. And honestly, last year wasn't much better. Robert Borden... well, he was just nasty."

Laith? Bullied? That didn't add up. Xander and Kanze, sure, but Laith was... Laith.

As if reading my thoughts, Victoria continued, "He was like a scrawny stray cat when he got here. He doesn't talk much about before, but whatever it was, wherever he came from..." She shook her head. "It wasn't good."

"It's hard to picture Laith scrawny." My face flushed as I realized I'd just admitted to checking out her maybe future husband's body.

"He's worked really hard," she said, either not noticing my faux pas or choosing to ignore it. "On his body. On his mind. Some people find freedom in shifting, but for Laith... I think he finally found a way to be in control."

Control. That was something I could understand. Hadn't everything I'd been planning before two wolves and a bear kidnapped me been about finally becoming the master of my own... fate?

"We should head back so you don't miss your meeting." Victoria shifted into a crouch, facing the entrance between the boulders. "But Remi?"

"Yeah?" I asked, still staring up at the moon.

"You don't have to be an ass about it like Laith, but do be in control."

I turned, furrowing my brows. "Of what?"

"Situations." She shrugged. "Choices. Once you let someone else decide what kind of person you are, it's hard to..." She swallowed thickly, like she was holding some emotion back. "Find your way out."

***

The clock above Ms. Shirley's counter read eight-oh-five when I arrived at the bookstore completely out of breath and aching from head to toe from the long, claustrophobic crawl back to the cavern and then the cross-campus sprint back to Therian Hall.

I peeked over the counter to see if Ms. Shirley was hiding back there like usual, but found only a note in Professor Helms' neat handwriting telling me to come on up. Nerves crackled in my stomach. When I had agreed to this meeting, I had still been desperately clinging to my belief that this was all just a dream. And in dreams, it's totally fine to let your hot professor become your private tutor in a subject that involves nudity.

But when it's real?

I shook away the suspicious thoughts. Just because Dean Mardone was a creeper, didn't mean Professor Helms was up to something shady. He was always so careful and polite with his female students. So conscientious. It was totally unfair for Laith and Victoria to imply he had ulterior motives for this meeting. They didn't even know him. He was a good man.

And besides, even if there was something *more* to the way he batted his eyelashes at me earlier, was it really that wrong when there was definitely something *more* on my end, too? We were both adults, and like five years apart tops.

I climbed the winding stairs to the attic, ducked under an extra layer of cobwebs someone had set out for Halloween, and found Professor Helms beaming at me from the other side of the glass faculty door. Instead of the stuffy faculty uniform, he wore skinny jeans and a T-shirt with an image of a giraffe wearing giant headphones and standing on top of a record player.

See? Just a normal twenty-something guy.

Who's a little more hipster than I expected, but fine, whatever.

Helms pushed the door open and waved me in. As I squeezed past him, he let the door close and for a brief second, I felt the brush of his arm across my shoulders. A warm shiver—*not a prickle*—ran down my back.

"Is this too weird?" Helms gestured at his clothing. "I thought my uniform might cause, ah, undue pressure, but now I fear I've gone too far in the opposite direction."

My eyes traveled down the length of his body, admiring the way the jeans fit him, the way the T-shirt subtly showed off the ridges of muscle underneath. "No, you look great," I said in a breathy tone that made me cringe. "I mean, you look really chill."

He grinned with his dimples. "I see. Very good. And you as well." He swallowed. "I mean, you look really chill."

I shrugged inside my cavernous hoodie and tucked a strand of hair behind my ears. "I assure you it is a carefully constructed act."

He laughed. "Mine too."

Our eyes met. We were standing very close, but it was a tiny stairwell after all. He cleared his throat and stepped back, gesturing to the spiral stairs.

"Let's go down to my office and chill, shall we?"

My stomach tensed. He was British. He probably wasn't up to date on American slang. He was definitely not asking me to come down to his office and, you know, *chill.*

I followed him down the spiral stairs into a large open area on the tower's second floor. The curtains were drawn, but there were several warm lamps lighting the space, one for each desk lined up along the walls.

"Only Deans get private offices. The rest of us have to share," Helms said, leaning against a desk with a framed photo of the golden wolf I'd seen him shifted into during Wolf Music. I couldn't decide if that was vanity, or curiosity. Would I keep a picture of my wolf around once I got her back?

"It's nice," I said, hugging myself awkwardly because I suddenly didn't know where I should stand or sit or if I was going to have to take any clothes off.

He smiled, and then all the spirit seemed to go out of him and he sagged against his desk. He ran a hand through his tousled hair. "Remi, darling, I have a confession to make."

My face tingled pleasantly when he called me darling. It was nothing at all like the possessive way Mardone called Laith *kitten*. It was just polite. And British. It took me a moment to remember to be concerned about his confession.

"Sir?" I asked.

He grimaced. "Oh, no, don't do that. Not when I'm dressed like this! It's Daniel. Please."

Daniel. I rolled his name around inside my head. It was a nice name.

"Do you remember the day we met?" Daniel asked, and I wondered why he phrased it that way, instead of saying the first day of class.

"Of course," I said. "I guess we've come full circle, huh? I needed you to save me from my shift, and now I need you to save my shift."

His smile didn't reach his eyes. "Yes. Well. About that, darling. You see, I'm afraid..." He paced away from the desk and then back. "I was only trying to reverse that one shift. But it seems I may have..."

Realization struck me like a slap from Dean Embry's grizzly paw. The way my skin would feel like a million hairs were trying to crawl out, the way my muscles felt like they would explode from the wolf's frantic pressure, the way every time I tried to let it out, it immediately vanished.

"Reversed them all," I whispered.

"I am *so* sorry, Remi." He moved closer, hands clasped in front of him. "Can you ever forgive me?"

My mind raced and my stomach twisted. All this time I thought I was broken... and I was. But it wasn't my fault.

"Why didn't you say something sooner?"

He ran both hands over his head, tugging at his hair. "I just... I didn't put two and two together. I supposed I was overly confident in my skills. Remi, I feel terrible. To think you might have been..." He turned away, shoulder slumping. "I'll understand if you want to tell the Gladwells what I did."

What would happen to him? It was an accident, but what if they thought he'd done it on purpose? That was absurd, of course. The man was clearly racked with regret. But would they see that? What if they sent him to the pound?

"No," I said quickly. "I'm not going to do that. As long as you can fix it."

His shoulder lifted and he turned to face me. Relief made him look even more boyish, maybe even five years younger. "Yes, of course. That's why I asked you to come here. Obviously."

I nodded, letting out the breath I'd been holding. "Okay. How do we do this?"

He moved closer. "I'll need to go inside your head again, if I may?"

"Whatever you need to do." I squared my shoulders and lifted my jaw.

He moved even closer, until the air between us sizzled with anticipation. I was going to get my wolf back.

"I'll need to touch you," he said softly. "Will that be alright?"

I laughed softly. *So polite.* "You don't always have to ask." I bit my lip. "Daniel."

His fingers closed around my skull and warmth spilled down my neck and shoulders. He flashed his dimples, just inches away from my face. "Right then. Can't be too careful about these things."

CHAPTER FOURTEEN

The monster stared out of the mirror, its bright green human eyes panicking between its large, pointed ears and long upper snout while its lower human jaw grimaced in pain.

I lifted the pewter-gray mask onto the top of my head, wincing at the mean red lines it left along my cheeks.

Now that's what I call sexy.

Aside from that the fact that I was never going to wear one anyway, all of Xander's goofy group costume ideas had been rendered moot three days ago when every student on campus received a gift bag containing formal evening attire and a stylized animal mask to match their inner beast.

The Halloween Ball would be a masquerade, and even though the nerds had at first been aghast at the prospect of wearing tuxedos instead of wizard robes, they had quickly cheered up when they realized my anti-costume stance had been thwarted by the mandatory masked attendance policy.

At least the rest of me looks great.

I twirled in front of the mirror, admiring the way the silver ball gown billowed around my ankles. And I had to hand it to the ravenous wolf still trapped inside me—I was doing a much better job filling out the low-cut bodice than I would have eight weeks ago after scraping cold beans out of a can all summer. A smile spread across my face.

If he hasn't noticed me yet, he will tonight.

But I knew he had noticed me.

I just didn't know what to do about it.

Nothing, Remi. He's your teacher.

But he wouldn't always be my teacher. And, actually, he was my *professor*, and wasn't that really a totally different thing? Even the Chancellor himself had said that we were both adults when he signed off on our private lessons. If you listened to those words just right, didn't they even sound a little bit like permission?

We'd met every weeknight since that first session, each one ending with his agonized apologies. None of his attempts to reverse the reverse shift had worked yet, and, frankly, that was fine by me. The fear of failure still fluttered somewhere in the back of my mind, but shifting would bring an end to our private lessons, and that would mean no more long talks about his own academy days, no more dimpled smiles after my jokes, no more gentle hands massaging all the tension right out of my head.

I wasn't ready to let go of that. I mean, I'd almost completely forgotten to prickle when I felt Laith's hazel eyes judging me from across Mardone's classroom.

Almost.

Sighing, I pulled my mask down over my face, slipped on the heels that had arrived with the gown, and left the quiet of my room. The second-floor hallway was empty, but the sounds of laughter and running water from the community bathroom told me I wasn't the only one running late for the Ball.

Black and orange streamers spiraled around the banister overlooking the Great Hall, and I paused there to take in the view. The furniture had been pushed to the edges of the room, creating a massive dance floor that swirled with colorful dresses and silk capes as couples waltzed to the classical sounds of a string quartet. Every face was hidden behind a mask, some of which were incredibly realistic with sculpted fangs and tufts of fur, while others were wildly impressionistic with feathers and sequins. Magical had never been a word I put any stock in, but even I had to admit there was really no other adjective that fit.

A man in a champagne tuxedo stood near the white-clothed buffet table, his shoulders draped with a royal blue cape that shimmered under the warm glow of the giant chandelier. His normally tousled blond hair was slicked back, away from the ornate golden wolf mask that obscured the upper half of his face.

My breath caught. Somehow my absent-minded professor had shifted into a dashing prince. As if sensing my gaze, the golden mask tilted upward, and Daniel lifted one hand in a beckoning wave.

Does he know who I am? My heart hammered against my ribs, or maybe it just felt that way due to the snugness of my dress.

Hiking up the skirt portion, I kicked off my heels and carried them down the stairs. Victoria's internship had her traveling tonight—someone somewhere had shifted on their eighteenth birthday last weekend and they had to be found—so if I fell on my ass, there'd be no one to pick me up. Once I safely reached the first floor, I slipped them back on, took a deep breath to settle the butterflies the golden wolf had stirred up, and then stepped into the ballroom.

Right into Winter Davenport's back.

Damn, it's hard to see in this mask!

Winter turned, blue eyes squinting through her delicate white wolf mask. Feathers plumed around its ears like tufts of fur, and a line of pale blue sequins ran up its muzzle and branched out over both eye holes. She looked like a bride in her gauzy white gown, a royal bride once you took into account the fur-lined red cape she wore.

No fair! I could have rocked a cape!

The white wolf mask's nose pointed down at my chest. "Wow, James. As an unwilling victim of your flashing fetish, I don't recall you being quite so well-endowed in August." She looked up, smiling sweetly and batting her eyelashes behind the mask. "The quads are really making a difference."

Really? That's *what you're still going with?*

I faked a sympathetic expression. "Oh, Winter, I'm so sorry. Didn't Derek tell you?" I rested my hand on her shoulder. "It's actually quints."

Her lips puckered under the shadow of her mask's nose, and then smoothed into one of her cruel smiles. "Just try to keep your dress on, okay? I promise there are other ways to get attention in life."

She whirled away, swinging her cape like an evil queen from some fairy tale movie. I watched her stalk over to the buffet table where Derek was filling his plate with Halloween-themed finger foods. Unlike all the other guys in the room, he had no cape to go with his gray tuxedo, and I realized she'd stolen hers from him. They argued briefly, and then she ripped the plate right out of his hands and disappeared into the crowd.

"Quints, huh?" Laith's voice rumbled quietly next to my ear. "You're hiding them well."

The prickles hit me so hard and so fast that I instinctively clutched at the shoulders of my gown—as if that would really keep it on during a shift.

He laughed, swinging around in front of me and mimicking my protective pose. "What the hell is this?"

"You scared me," I growled, leaving my arms folded like they were because I really didn't want him to see my heaving chest right now. "For Christmas, I'm getting you a collar with a bell on it."

He bit his lip, and the copper cougar mask rose with the lifting of his human eyebrows underneath it. "You're into some weird stuff, St. James. But I can dig it."

"You can dig it?" I scoffed. "What are you, sixty? You sound like the Chancellor."

He drew his black cape across the human half of his face. "I wear many disguises, Remi," he said in a fair representation of the Chancellor's dorky dad drawl.

Rolling my eyes, I pushed him out of my way. "If you'll excuse me."

He fell in step beside me. "What's the rush? Got a hot date with the geek fleet?"

"No," I said, intending to leave it at that, but my head flicked automatically toward the golden wolf talking to a bear-masked woman whose sturdy shape I recognized as Dean Belhollow.

"Ah." Laith's lips pressed into a flat line. "You're barking up the wrong tree, Poodle."

I sighed. "Once again, no one asked for your opinion, Mister Whiskers."

He grunted. "It's not an opinion, it's a fact. Professors shouldn't—"

I stopped and planted my fists on my hips, not caring that we were now in the middle of the dance floor. "Was there something you needed from me, Laith, or are you just trying to ruin my night?"

Hazel eyes gazed steadily at me from behind the copper mask. The cougar's nose was wrinkled up in a snarl that made it difficult to tell whether Laith's actual expression was equally angry or not.

"I thought that since we were both flying solo this evening, you might consider doing Victoria the favor of guarding my virtue from Lecherous Lenore, but I can see now that you've planned a very busy evening making googly eyes at the guy responsible for your grade, so... I'll leave you to it."

Then, for the second time in ten minutes, someone spun away from me with a ridiculous, dramatic swish of their cape. But this time I hated to see that person go.

And that was all the more reason to focus my crush energy on Daniel Helms. These stupid impossible feelings for Laith Brighton needed to be stamped out once and for all.

"Hey, Remi! Over here!" Winter's voice rang out in the sugary-sweet, sing-song tone she normally only used to torment me in front of professors.

I turned toward it against my better judgment and found her sitting on one of the couches against the wall, sandwiched between two boys in wolf masks, who were eagerly chowing down on bone-shaped sandwiches from the plate I'd watched her take from Derek.

The visible halves of my nerds' faces at least had the good sense to look sheepish when I clomped over to them as fast as my heels would carry me.

"What the hell is this?" I demanded, and my heart twinged, remembering Laith's delighted smile when he made fun of me with the same words just moments ago.

"Oh, hey, Remi," Xander squeaked. Kanze waved.

Winter smiled, teeth flashing beneath her wolf mask's sequined muzzle. "Listen, Remi, I've been talking to the boys, and I don't want you to worry about a thing. They are *more* than welcome to join my pack."

"Excuse me?" I snarled, fists clenching at my sides.

The boys shrank into the couch, but Winter's lips pushed into a pout. "Don't be angry, Remi. I'm only trying to give you peace of mind."

"Peace of mind?" I sputtered. "How would stealing my pack give me peace of mind, exactly?"

"Well, I mean..." she lowered her voice to a stage whisper, "since you aren't going to be here much longer."

My fingernails dug into my palms and I gritted my teeth. One day, I would rip her throat out, but it wouldn't be with my human mouth. "I'm not going anywhere."

Winter made her blue eyes big behind the mask. "So you're shifting again? That's wonderful news!"

"Remi, that's amazing!" Xander shouted, drawing several stares. He lowered his voice. "When did it happen?"

I could feel my face turning as red as Winter's stupid cape, so I ducked my head and stared at the hem of my gown, rustling just above my heels. "It hasn't. Yet."

Xander's face fell. "Oh."

"But it will," I said firmly. "And soon. I'm not going to fail. I'm not going anywhere."

"I admire your determination, Remi," Winter said, sliding the plate onto Kanze's lap and getting to her feet. She touched my elbow. "But if it doesn't work out, my offer still stands. I'll take good care of the boys. In fact…" Her eyes lit up and she turned back to the couch. "You know, my friends Jadice and Kamilla were looking for dance partners. Maybe you'd like to come find them with me?"

Xander's jaw dropped. Kanze set the plate aside and scrambled to his feet.

I threw my hands up in the air. "Are you kidding me?"

Kanze glared at me from behind his silver mask. "Were *you* going to dance with us?"

"If you want to dance, Remi—" Xander started, jumping up.

"You know what?" I pushed my hands toward them. "Go for it. I hope you thoroughly enjoy whatever bizarrely cruel prank Winter has planned for you."

Winter gave me a pitying look. "I know this must be difficult for you, Remi, but there's no need to take it out on your friends." She looped her arms through *my* nerds' elbows. "Come on, guys. You're too cute to be wallflowers."

CHAPTER FIFTEEN

I'm *too cute to be a wallflower*, I thought for the hundredth time in the hour since I'd planted myself on the couch and shamelessly devoured the rest of the food from Derek's plate. Even the grotesque meatballs with spaghetti spider legs.

But I made no move to get back out there and mingle. I didn't want to watch Xander and Kanze going over to the dark side. I didn't want to risk Laith being the only person to ask me for a dance that would mean nothing even while it drove my body to cellular meltdown.

I should just go back to my room.

Behind the mask, my eyes felt sore around the edges, and not just from the tight threads holding it in place. I hadn't exactly been crying during my time on the couch, but I hadn't exactly *not* been crying either. Standing on the balcony earlier, I had let myself believe the one thing I never allowed myself to believe—that something *magical* might happen before the night was over. Now it just seemed like part of a dream I'd been rudely woken up from before it ever really got started.

I gathered my dress up so I wouldn't step on it when I stood, but a shadow fell across my lap, making me look up. Warm brown eyes peered down the golden wolf's nose and a worried expression tightened the lower human half of Daniel's face.

"Remi? That *is* you, isn't it, darling?"

"It's me." I forced a laugh. "Just another gray wolf in the crowd. Except, you know, not."

"You're not just another..." He sank onto the couch next to me, but a respectable distance away. He rested his elbows on his knees and his chin on his clasped fists. "We're going to fix it. I promise."

"When?" I threw up my hands. "I'm running out of time. I got an F on my Practical Shifting midterm, and a D in the P.E. part of Health and P.E. because I can't join in any of the werewolf games."

Why am I picking a fight with him right now?

"Soon. I can feel it, darling." He reached over as if he were going to place his hand on my knee, then pulled it back. "We're almost there."

I stared at his hand. *Almost where?*

He tilted his head. "Is that the only thing bothering you?"

I snorted and flung a hand toward the dance floor. "Winter stole my pack."

Daniel shook his head. "She can't do that. Packs are set."

"But if I get kicked out..."

He *did* place his hand on my knee then. Warmth shot up my leg, straight to my brain, and I could have sworn the chandelier over the dance floor brightened. A flash of red caught my attention, but it wasn't Winter's cape. It was Dean Mardone's hair snuggled up under Laith's chin as they swayed in place like this was a high school homecoming dance and not a formal masquerade ball.

The Dean's eyes were shut blissfully tight and the fabric of Laith's bronze tuxedo bunched under her grasping fingers. A pang of guilt flashed through me for not taking him seriously earlier. That woman was a shameless predator.

Laith's dead-looking eyes landed on mine. They darted to the golden wolf beside me, and then away from us completely. I knew what he must be thinking, but this was not the same. Daniel was a good man. Nothing like Lenore Mardone.

"Ah! Looks like it's professor's choice?" Daniel said, turning his hand palm up on my knee. "Shall we?"

Fireworks exploded inside my chest as I laced my fingers through his and let him pull me to my feet, drowning out any alarm bells that might have accompanied his total misreading of the Laith/Lenore situation

He didn't lead me out onto the dance floor, but drew me close right where we stood, gently placing his other hand on my waist. Our chests brushed as we both started out on the wrong foot, and we let them stay that way once we finally got the hang of things.

"I was never very good at this," he said softly. "My ex always said I had four left feet."

I swallowed. "Your ex?"

His thumb caressed the back of my hand. "Have I not mentioned her?"

I remembered him saying something that first day in class. After I asked my embarrassing question about wolves mating for life. But I shook my head because I wanted to know more about the person he was probably imagining in my place.

"Ah, well. Nothing interesting to tell, really. We were together, and then we weren't. Same old story." He shrugged the shoulder that my hand rested on.

"When did you break up?" I wasn't sure I really wanted to know, but it seemed like he wanted to talk about it. Just my luck.

He twirled me like a ballerina and then brought me close again. "That's the funny thing, I suppose. We never did. After graduation, she just stopped talking to me. I don't even know where she is."

"We call that ghosting," I said.

His wolf mask's nose bumped against mine. "All for the best I suppose."

And then we stopped dancing.

He lifted his mask, and he had the same painful red lines I had seen in the mirror earlier, but his eyes shone with warmth and... something maybe sort of like desire. A shiver ran down my back.

Is this really happening?

"All I'm saying, Remi, is that I know what it's like to feel rejected." His breath felt warm on my cheek.

"But sometimes those just weren't the people we needed to accept us."

My blood pounded in my ears. A tingling sensation raced through every vein in my body. Daniel's hand grazed my cheek on its way to push my mask up onto my forehead. Our human faces were suddenly very, very close together.

A guttural, off-key howl ripped through the night, and I jerked away from Daniel's parted lips, searching for what seemed likely to be a drunken source.

Daniel's fingers pressed into the small of my back. "What is it, Remi?"

"Didn't you hear...?"

My words trailed off. The sound of bubbling water faded into my ears, as though someone were slowly turning the volume up.

Daniel and I were no longer in the Great Hall. We were in the alcove under the tower, in the dark corner farthest from both the main entrance and the bookstore. I twisted my head to the left and there was the magnificent fountain, its enormous spray of water glittering in the moonlight. The three animal statues had their backs to us.

How? When?

Another discordant howl rang out, and I startled backward out of Daniel's grip. "Don't you hear that howling?"

His brow furrowed. "No one is howling, Remi. Are you feeling alright?"

I turned away from him, stepping out of the alcove and onto the driveway that looped around the fountain. I cocked my head, straining for another sound. *Something is out there.* My heels clicked on the cobblestones as I ventured further away from the building.

"Remi! Where on earth are you going?" Daniel caught up with me, laying his hand on the small of my back, but much lower than he had before.

I twisted away from him. "Whoa, hey, no. What are you doing?"

Both of his arm snapped back to his sides and he lowered his eyes. "My apologies. I seem to have misread... something."

"Misread *what*?" I snapped, my eyes darting to the main entrance, which suddenly seemed a long ways off. My palms twitched with an urge to hit all fours and run.

Daniel glanced up at me through his thick eyelashes. "Well, in my office, darling. I asked... and you said I didn't *need* to ask..."

My lip curled up in disgust. "That is not what I meant!"

He smiled and batted those long eyelashes. "But... wasn't it?"

A snarl bubbled up louder than the fountain, and I whipped toward it and the motionless bronze beasts. "How can you not *hear* that?"

"Remi, there's nothing out there." He came up behind me again, this time touching my shoulder.

I pushed his hand away. "Dude. *Stop.* I need some space here."

Daniel took a step back, bowing his head. "As you wish."

I lifted my hands to my head, which was practically vibrating with the volume of the now persistent growling. "Why can't you hear this?!"

"Because there's nothing to hear." His brow creased. "Tell me, did you have anything to drink this evening, darling?"

"Don't call me that!"

"I'm sorry. I'm, ah, just a little confused here. You have to understand..."

"I don't *have* to understand anything." My hands fell to my sides, fingers curling into the fabric of my skirt. The sound had become a series of short, choppy howls bouncing off the walls of my skull.

An alarm call.

It was *me*.

My wolf.

Even though she was still on the other side of some insurmountable barrier, I felt her power coursing through my veins. My eyes lifted slowly, taking in the man in the champagne tuxedo, his silly blue cape twisted limply to one side. His golden mask sat on his forehead, nose pointing up at the sky, revealing its empty plastic interior.

"Daniel." I took a step forward, my eyes locked on his. "Why don't I remember coming outside?"

Daniel looked around with a confused quirk to his lips. "I asked if you wanted to get some, ah, fresh air. Remember? You said yes, and I helped you down the steps because you were tripping over your skirt. And then we had another dance, and then we... well, it seemed that we were.... perhaps, ah, going to... well, anyway, I see now that I was wrong."

The hapless stammer that had always seemed so charming suddenly seeming like a glaring affectation.

I shook my head and rolled my eyes. "I'm going back inside."

He lowered his head as though he were going to respect that, but the moment I passed by him, his hand shot out and clutched my arm.

"I wish you wouldn't do that, darling," he murmured, and his breath wafted right into my nose.

My recoil nearly brought us both to the ground, but his fingers tightened on my elbow, holding me up as he planted his feet. I flung my head away from the putrid stench flowing from his lungs as my own seized up, coughing as though they were full of smoke. My stomach heaved and I spit bile onto the cobblestones.

"You see, Remi, you're not feeling very well," Daniel growled, fighting to keep hold of my arm as I wrenched it this way and that.

"It was you," I gasped.

The truth flickered behind my eyes with every breath. The first time we met. The empty stairwell. His fingers around my head. He hadn't botched reversing my shift. He had purposefully caged my wolf.

"You son of a—" I sank my human teeth into the fingers gripping my arm.

He yelped and stumbled back, doubling over and clutching his bleeding knuckles with the hem of his cape. But a crazed grin spread across his face.

"It's true then," he panted. "You have the gift."

I stepped backward, kicking out of my heels because it was clear now I would need to make a run for the door. "I don't know what you're talking about."

"Oh, I think you do." He straightened up, flinging his cape back into place. "Forgive me for eavesdropping, but I overheard you talking to Ms. Shirley in the bookstore. I've found that young women do have a tendency to lie..." His lip curled in disgust. "So, I had to find out for myself."

I remember his arms lifting me up the stairs that day. I'd just assumed it had been good timing, but no. He had been lying in wait.

My hero, my ass.

My eyes darted to the entrance, calculating my chances of outrunning him in my stupid gown. I would have given anything to be stuck with two nerds in a three-headed dog suit right then.

"You could run, yes," Daniel—*No, let's go back to Helms*—said. "But wouldn't you rather stay and find out why poor Ms. Shirley warned you not to tell?"

"I don't have anything to tell," I growled. "So no, I'd rather get back inside with my friends."

"Your *friends*?" He scoffed. "The ones who abandoned you the first time a prettier girl gave them a better offer?"

"Nice try." I rolled my eyes. "But finding out you prefer blondes, too, isn't exactly going to break my heart, all things considered." I hiked my skirt up to my ankles. "I'm going inside now. You can follow... if you want me to scream."

He leapt forward with lightning reflexes, blocking my path. "You're not safe here, Remi," he said softly, fluttering his eyelashes. "Come with me back to Hawtrey. Unless you fancy the idea of spending your golden years blind and sniffing out books?"

"Get *out* of my way."

He grasped me by the elbows, and his words tumbled out so quickly and quietly I could barely understand him. "The scent-sight is the only way to locate a young shifter before he turns into a wolf in the middle of the grocer's. Ms. Shirley is the youngest one left in the U.S. If they find out you can sniff, it won't matter if you graduate. They'll *never* let you leave. Do you understand me?" He shook me a little. "You will become a slave, Remi."

A rectangle of light opened up over Helms' shoulder, and a tall shadow with two round ears on top of his head stood in the middle of the warm glow.

"That you, St. James?" Laith called.

"Yes!" I hated the way my voice cracked. "It's me!"

"Sorry to interrupt, but would you mind coming inside?" His silhouette leaned against the doorframe. "We've got a developing situation on the dance floor. Your pack mates are trying to get a macarena going." He shuddered. "It's not good."

"Oh no! Be right there!" I called, pulling against Helms' grip.

Helms' mouth flattened into a tight line and he dropped my arms, turning to face Laith with a flourish of his cape. "While that does sound dismal, Mr. Brighton, Remi and I were on the verge of a breakthrough with her, ah, little problem."

"In an evening gown?" Laith came down the steps, letting the door slam shut behind him, his own black cape billowing behind him.

"The beast does what it will." Helms shrugged, but I caught the way he squared his shoulders and planted his feet. "Isn't that right, Remi?"

Laith sauntered to the edge of the alcove under the tower. "Yeah, I bet he does."

"I'm not quite sure I like what you're imply—"

"You feeling shifty, St. James? I can leave you be, but..." He jerked a thumb over his shoulder. "Seriously. You're their alpha."

Really? I am?

Wait, not important right now.

My toes curled against the cobblestone, ready to make my run for it. "No, I'm not feeling shifty. At all."

Laith stepped out from under the tower, and his copper cougar mask snarled in the moonlight. He held out his hand. "Well then, how about you come on over here?"

Helms lunged and shreds of champagne fabric flew through the air. The golden wolf's paws hit the ground only once before it slammed into Laith's chest, knocking him backward into the shadows under the tower.

I dashed toward the terrible snarling tangle of human and animal limbs rolling around on the porch. *Shift, Laith! Why isn't he shifting?!*

The golden wolf, still draped in the blue cape, straddled Laith's torso, snapping its jaws in the air as Laith gripped the sides of its head, holding it off his throat. I leapt the last few feet, crashing onto my knees in the billows my gown, but I caught the hem of the cape and yanked as hard as I could.

The wolf coughed, but kept straining against the little golden rope that held the cape around a neck that was much thicker than Helms' human one. His teeth flashed next to Laith's nose, even as the veins in Laith's forearms seemed to bulge with the effort of holding the wolf off.

Why won't he shift?!

I hauled back on the cape again, and then pulled, hand over hand, bunching the blue silk up in my lap until the golden wolf's forepaws were in the air, only the tips of his claws scrabbling against the concrete. White foam dripped from the edges of his mouth and his eyes began to roll.

When Helms caught on to me, he must have realized there was only one way to ease the tension on the cape. With what must have been his last reserve of strength, he wrenched his head out of Laith's hands and sprang for me.

But Laith's legs, which had been trapped up under the weight of the wolf, unfurled with tremendous force and struck the wolf square in the ribs, spinning him around mid-air. The cape wrapped itself around Helms' throat and I jerked one more time.

Helms landed on the cobblestones with a heavy thud.

He didn't move.

Laith crawled over to me, flinging his mask aside. "Are you okay?"

I couldn't tear my eyes off the limp wolf.

Did I kill him?

Laith's fingers brushed my shoulder, but he pulled them back. "Remi, are you okay? Can you look at me?"

"Is he dead?" I whispered.

Laith leaned forward, pressing two fingers to the wolf's neck. He shook his head and dug the fingers under the twisted cape, loosening it. "He's alive."

My eyes finally gave up their hold on the wolf and found Laith's face, his hazel eyes wet with... *With tears?*

"Are *you* okay? Why didn't you shift? Did he break you, too?"

"I didn't shift because I would have killed him." His brow furrowed. "What do you mean 'break me, too'?"

"It was him. He's the reason..." My hands gripped the blue cape. "He did something to me."

Laith's eyes widened in horror. His hands came up like he was going to touch me, but, once again, he pulled them back. His voice came out low and deadly. "What did he do to you?"

I shook my head. "No, no, not like that... I mean, maybe he would've if..." My voice hitched, but I shoved those feelings back down for now. "My wolf, Laith. He did something to my wolf. It's like... he locked her up."

Laith's eyes fluttered shut and he sat back on his haunches. He rapped a fist against his skull. "Stupid. Why didn't I—?"

I grabbed his wrist before he could do that again. "Whoa, what?"

"I should've known." He settled for tugging at his hair. "Remi, I'm so sorry."

"What the hell are you talking about?" My head hurt. My heart hurt. The last thing I needed right now was to be reassuring Laith that something that obviously wasn't his fault was... not his fault.

Laith kicked a foot against the unconscious wolf's back. "He's a Manip. I should have sensed it right away."

"I have no idea what that is." I laughed, even though nothing was really funny. "Or why that makes this about you."

"Because..." Laith dragged his fingers down the side of his face.

But before he could explain, a set of double doors slammed open, bathing us all in light—a girl in a torn ball gown, a guy in a ripped tuxedo, and a shifted professor lifeless on the ground.

CHAPTER SIXTEEN

The doors slammed shut.

A pair of heels clicked toward us in the darkness, accompanied by the swish of fabric moving quickly over concrete. My breaths stumbled all over each other in my throat until my lungs, unsure which ones were coming and which ones were going, shut the whole thing down. My chest froze up with the rest of me.

How will we ever explain this?

Laith scrambled to his feet. "Dean—"

Dean Mardone swept him aside with one arm and knelt beside me, creating an unsettling puddle of dark red fabric next to Helms' prone form. She laid her fingers against his furry throat, as Laith had just done. Her eyelids closed and her shoulders sagged with relief.

"Well, you haven't killed him." She lifted her mask and her fierce green eyes traveled the length of Helms' blue cape, from the part twisted around his neck to the folds still gathered in my lap. "But it certainly seems like you tried."

"Dean Mardone—" Laith tried again.

She held up a silencing hand and hissed into my face, "What have you dragged Laith into, you shiftless little—"

"Lenore!" Laith roared.

Mardone's gaze flicked upward. "Not now, Lai—"

"He's a Manip," Laith spat. "Helms is a Manip."

Mardone's lips parted, but no sound came out. Slowly, her eyes slid back to where her fingers still rested on Helms' neck. His left paw twitched, and she yanked her hand back as though he were a venomous snake.

"No. Impossible." She shook her head. "He's just a wolf."

"Rare," Laith said, folding his arms over his chest. "Not impossible."

Mardone held up her hand, and Laith obediently helped her up, but she didn't release her hold on him.

"This is a serious accusation, Laith," she murmured, almost into his neck. "One that could easily backfire. Are you *sure*?"

Laith disentangled his fingers from her grip, but his eyes remain locked on hers. "He bound Remi's wolf."

Mardone gasped, the tiny sound of a particularly tricky puzzle piece clicking into place. "Do you have proof?"

Laith gestured at me. "Remi says—"

"Remi *says*." Mardone let out a harsh laugh. "That's your proof? A shiftless girl with a shameless crush *says* a professor manipulated her? Come on, Laith, you're smarter than that. We all saw them dancing. Who's to say he didn't dash her dreams and she responded like..." she gestured at me and the cape and the still wolf, "... like some kind of feral?"

"Hey!" I struggled to stand without help, but I was tangled in what suddenly felt like miles and miles of silk. "That's not... I'm not... *ugh*! Whose idea was this stupid masquerade anyway?!"

Laith offered me his hand, and since I didn't want to spend the rest of the night being talked over like I wasn't even there, I grabbed it.

Bad idea, Remi.

The moment our palms touched, a flurry of prickles shot up my arm, and Laith's wrist stiffened like he'd received a jolt. The second I was steady on my legs, he dropped my hand and wiped his own on his pants. It was definitely the first time I'd ever found myself hoping my hands were just grotesquely sweaty, but the furtive glance he darted down at his open palm before stuffing it in his pocket left me worried.

Worse, Dean Mardone's shrewdly arched eyebrows and pursed lips told me none of it had been lost on her.

"I'm not feral," I snapped. "And I don't even know what a Manip *is*. Those are Laith's words, not mine. And yeah, maybe I should have called B.S. on a *professor* asking a *student* to dance, but that doesn't make it okay that I can't even remember how he got me outside. And don't you *dare* ask if I was drinking! I haven't had a drop of *anything* all night, and... and... and I'm actually really, *really* thirsty right now!"

I knew I hadn't really stuck the landing of that speech, but the rush of words had made me acutely aware of the sandy, cactus-filled desert formerly known as my throat. A cough right then would have almost certainly produced a tumbleweed.

Mardone turned her chin toward Laith, but her eyes stayed on me. "Any old shifter—well, not a *bear*, of course—could cause time loss on that scale. You've no proof he's a Manip."

"Did you not *hear* me?" Laith growled. "He bound her—"

"Helms trapped my wolf," I cut Laith off, because as much as I appreciated him showing up when he did, I was perfectly capable of telling my own story. And even though I would have much rather been talking to the Vice-Chancellor or Belhollow, the words poured out of me. Everything I knew about Helms from that first day in the stairwell to the moment he shifted with intent to kill.

Well, almost everything.

The two warnings about my scent-sight swirled in my mind. First, Ms. Shirley's, which I had blindly followed without questioning because I hadn't felt it was a plot thread much worth following in the crazy dream I believed I was having at the time, and then Helms' tonight, which I would have blindly ignored as just another part of his ploy to isolate me had it not reminded me to be worried about Ms. Shirley's warning now that I knew this was all *really* happening.

So I left that part out.

When I was finished telling her how Helms had tried to rip out Laith's throat, Dean Mardone looked at me with something almost like admiration. "So you strangled him."

I lifted my chin. "Yes."

A faint smile twitched the edge of Mardone's bright red lips. "Perhaps I've underestimated you, Miss St. James." She turned back to Laith, her eyes hard. "You could have been killed. Why didn't you shift?"

Laith's back straightened. "I didn't have time."

Mardone laughed. "The truth, please?"

Laith's jaw flexed. "Because I knew there wouldn't be anything left of him if I did."

"Well, it certainly would have been easier to open and shut this case if you had." She sighed and shook her head. "Go up to my office and lock the door. Don't come out until I come for you. I'll take care of..." she waved her hand at Helms, whose ears were twitching, "... all this."

"Yes, ma'am," Laith said, reaching for my hand.

I yanked it away. "No way. I'm not going anywhere until the Gladwells get here."

Whatever admiration Mardone may have felt for me a moment earlier dried up in an instant. She smiled at me with utter condescension. "I suppose you haven't spent enough time as a wolf to understand this, but if another wolf—*any* wolf—walks out those doors and sees Professor Helms like this, the pack mind may very well take over. Laith could be ripped limb from limb."

I opened my mouth to protest, but Laith's fingers brushed mine. "She's right, Remi," he said, and there was real fear trembling at the edges of my name. "We need to go. She'll take care of us. *Both of us.*" He gave her a hard look.

"What are you going to do?" I demanded, stomach turning. "Finish him off?"

"Don't be ridiculous!" Dean Mardone rolled her eyes like that was the stupidest thing she'd ever heard. "There's no hiding a body from dogs."

***

A spiral-horned skull hanging on the wall behind Mardone's desk glowed blue in the light from her computer. Laith shut the door behind us, turning the lock with a soft click, as I felt along the wall for a light switch.

"Don't," he whispered, and then added, "I'm sorry. I know you've probably been alone in the dark with enough jerks for one night."

"For one lifetime," I muttered, rubbing the goosebumps that had popped up on my arms. "But I'm going to trust Victoria's judgment on this one."

"She wouldn't steer you wrong."

Laith crossed the room and plopped down in Mardone's swiveling leather chair. The computer washed his features in the same eerie light that lit up the leering skull. I noticed for the first time he had a dark smudge over his left eye.

"You're bleeding." I touched what would be the same spot on my own forehead.

His brow furrowed and he winced. He touched the spot and then examined his fingertips. "Nah. Not anymore. What about you? All in one piece?"

"I'm afraid to ever look at my knees again, but yeah, I think so, basically."

On the outside anyway.

"That was pretty bad ass." The chair squeaked as he leaned back, grinning. "The thing with the cape."

I grimaced. I really didn't want to think about it— the weight of the wolf's body pulling at the other end, his paws scratching at the air, the foam bubbling from his mouth. Just because he technically deserved it didn't make the sense memories any less disturbing.

"That was a pretty impressive kick," I said, because I really didn't want to get into any of those feelings out loud right now.

Laith shrugged. His face grew serious. "We did what we had to do."

I wandered deeper into the room, standing behind one of the chairs in front of the desk, stroking the polished wood at the top. Angry voices filtered up from two stories below.

"What did she mean about the pack mind taking over?" I whispered. "Is that a real thing or just wolf-hating hyperbole?"

"Oh, it's real." Laith snorted. "What do you think all that wolf music crap is for?"

I still hadn't been able to participate in wolf music yet, obviously, but I'd sat through every three-hour long practice this semester, just watching and listening as all the other wolves on campus— students, professors, cafeteria workers, and groundskeepers—gathered in the amphitheater and howled at the moon. It didn't do much for me, but I remembered the way it had felt to howl with the

Gladwells in the limo, and the way I had once heard the stars sing.

My fingers gripped the back of the chair. "I thought it was just a weird choir."

"Yeah, a weird choir designed to make your relationship with all other wolves, not just your pack, the strongest bond in your life."

A shiver ran down my neck. "Pack minds, mental manipulators... they sure didn't advertise all this in the promo video."

Laith lifted his arms like, *What can you do?* "Come for the hot guy, stay for the gradual loss of free will."

Helms' warning echoed in my mind. *You will become a slave, Remi.*

A sharp howl rose up over the human voices outside. Laith's head tilted, listening, and his sharp angles looked even sharper in the dim blue light.

"Laith?"

"It's okay. Don't be afraid."

"I'm not," I snapped. "Well, I *am*, but not... I mean... are you safe in here with me? Could they make me hurt you?"

"One, a lone wolf would never stand a chance in a cat fight. Though I *am* still wearing this stupid cape..." He did the lip-biting thing that drove me crazy. "Two, pack mind isn't that precise. It's a blunt instrument. You'd have to actually *be* with the pack for it to really get to you. It barely even counts as a mental ability. More like extreme peer pressure."

I stepped around the chair I'd been strangling— *Just something I do now, I guess*—and sank into the plush seat. My gown puffed up all around me, and I smoothed it down, vowing to never wear a dress this elaborate again, maybe not even to my wedding.

"Laith?" I asked again.

This time, he just lifted his eyebrows and made a sound of acknowledgement.

"You said Helms bound my wolf." I played with one of the many tears in the fabric of my skirt. "And the way you said it... well, it sounded like some sort of known terminology. And Mardone reacted that way. But if..."

Laith leaned forward, resting his elbows on the desk. "Then why didn't anyone think of it sooner?"

I nodded.

Laith sighed and raked both hands through his hair. "What do you know about shifter mental powers?"

Like being able to see things with my nose? But I wasn't ready to tell anyone that secret yet.

"I know we can all communicate telepathically eventually, but I thought that was pretty much it."

Laith scratched the back of his head and chewed on his lip, not in the sexy way—okay, it was still sexy—but in an almost manic way.

"Okay. Well. There's a lot of stuff in between the basic telepathy even bears can manage and what a Manip like Helms can do. Things like laying fake scent trails to lure freshmen into the woods. Technically, that's a manipulation, too, but..." He drummed his fingers on the desk. "There's a sort of fail-safe mechanism with most mental abilities. You can't use them on another trained shifter without them knowing. So, for instance, you can't cheat on your mate and make them forget about it. They would feel you poking around in their head and hopefully dump you."

Another howl cut through the night, followed by two more. My eyes drifted over my shoulder to the door.

"It's locked, don't worry. Only Mardone's getting in here without knocking it down, and they'd have to recruit a bear to do that."

"Dean Embry's not my biggest fan."

Laith chuckled. I settled back in my chair and tried to ignore the sounds outside.

"You were saying?"

"Right." Laith cleared his throat. "So, a Manip is someone who can override that fail-safe. They can get inside another shifter's head without them ever knowing. And Helms... well, he probably wasn't just in your head, but the whole faculty's. That's why it never occurred to them."

Just thinking about that man—that *monster*—inside my head made my mouth taste like his rotten stench all over again. I must have been smacking my lips or making a face because Laith swiveled his chair around, opened a tiny fridge that had been hiding behind him, and swiveled back, tossing me a bottle of water. I unscrewed the cap and guzzled the cold liquid down.

"Remi," Laith said softly, "I need you to know how sorry I am. It should have occurred to me." He dropped his head into his hands.

I rested my bottle on the arm of my chair and swiped my arm across my wet lips. "You keep saying that, but I don't see why *you* should have known something even the Gladwells missed. You're not respons—"

His head jerked back, and he lifted a hand to stop me. He peered closer at the top of Mardone's desk, and then batted at her mouse, waking up the computer so it shed a brighter light. He lifted a piece of paper off the desk. It rattled in his hand.

"What the hell?" he muttered.

His eyes flew up to mine, as wide as the empty sockets of the skull on the wall.

"Tell me I'm reading this wrong."

I pushed out of my chair and went around to his side of the desk, leaning over his shoulder to see the piece of paper. A fancy letterhead at the top read: **Tooth & Claw Society.**

"What the hell?" he repeated. "I mean, what the *actual* hell?"

"Shhh, let me read it." I snatched the paper out of his hands and sat on the edge of the desk. "'To Dean Lenore Mardone, Gladwell Academy of Shifters. This year's deadline for submission of your dean's list is December twenty-first.'" I looked down at Laith. "That doesn't sound so bad."

"Keep reading," he said, voice strained.

I cleared my throat. "'The Tooth and Claw Society will make the final determination on all candidates for culling'... *Culling*?! Isn't that when—?"

He swallowed loud enough for me to hear. "When you weed out the weakest members of a herd."

"That has to be a typo." I turned the paper over like there would be some sort of explanation on the other side. "Being on a dean's list is a *good* thing."

Laith gave a dark laugh. "The only word I can think of even close to culling is killing. And that's the same damn thing."

"No. No way." I shook my head, laying the paper back down. "You can't honestly believe that's what this means. It has to be some sort of prank. The Tooth and Claw Society—that sounds like some kind of frat thing. What *is* that?"

"I don't know." He tapped his finger on the page. "But look at the names."

Underneath the typed letter was a list of handwritten names, most of which I only vaguely recognized, except for the one at the very bottom, in the biggest, angriest-looking scrawl:

Victoria Manuel

CHAPTER SEVENTEEN

The computer screen's glow washed the color from Laith's eyes. He held his jaw so tight that his cheeks had become two dark slashes of shadow. He didn't look like he'd seen a ghost; he looked like he'd *become* a ghost.

"Hey." I laid my hand on his shoulder, ignoring the tingling under my skin. "We're not going to let anything happen to her. And again, we can't even be sure this is bad. Words don't always mean the same things here as they do elsewhere. Shifting, for instance..."

Laith's hollow gaze drifted to my hand. "Why is that happening?"

I jolted back. "I'm sorry. I didn't mean anything by—"

Laith shook his head. "No. I didn't mean why are you touching me, I meant why does it always feel like *that* when you touch me?"

His words jolted me to the core, like that time I was staying on a farm with Foster Family #6 and walked straight into an almost invisible electric fence. It was the kind of shock that felt more like being walloped with a heavy stick. Equal parts painful and confusing. That was exactly what it was like to find out after all this time, that I had the same effect on Laith as he had on me.

But we were staring at a piece of paper that suggested his girlfriend, who was the closest thing I had to a best friend in this insane place, was being offered up like some sort of a sacrifice to a spooky-named secret society.

It was not the time to talk prickling.

There would *never* be a time to talk prickling.

My offending hand burrowed into the folds of my gown in lieu of a pocket to hide in. "I guess I don't know what you mean."

He groaned and massaged his temples. "I'm sorry. Long night. *Weird* night. Getting a little jumpy. What were you saying?"

"Just that we can't know for sure this means what it seems like it means. I mean, that would be insane. With all the money they spend on us? That doesn't add up."

Laith picked up the paper and studied it again. "Unless this Tooth and Claw Society... what if that's where all the money comes from?"

He jumped up, the chair rolling back into the little fridge. He yanked open the top left drawer and gestured to the right side where I perched. "Hurry. Search those. Anything with Tooth and Claw, or maybe just T and C."

"Laith!" I slid over, catching him by both wrists before he could start pawing through Mardone's staples and ink pens. "Let's just take some deep breaths. Watch the thoughts float by or whatever that is you hate me for not doing."

But Laith's eyes lit on something in the spot I'd just abandoned. He wriggled out of my grasp and pounced on a pile of manila folders I guess I'd been sitting on.

"Here. See what she says about this one." He pressed one of the student files into my hands and tore through the others, undoubtedly searching for Victoria's. There was no stopping him.

With a sigh, I opened the file in my hands. It was for a senior named Jake Powell, who I recognized from the photo clipped to the first page as this oddly scrawny senior bear I'd often seen sitting in the courtyard sketching anyone who would shift for him. I'd only ever known him by his nerd-given name of Creepy Crayon.

Flipping through seven semesters of lackluster grades, I finally came to a comments section where all of his professors had shared their notes about him. A lot of them were probably decipherable only to the person who'd written them, but Dean Mardone's handwriting was neater—and loopier—than most.

Daydreamer. Lacks focus and ambition. Mentally weak, even for a bear.

I double-checked his name against the list she was submitting to the Tooth and Claw Society. Sure enough, Jake Powell was there. Her unflattering notes lent little credence to my theory that this was actually some sort of honor they were being nominated for.

"Got it!" Laith said, dodging around me to hold Victoria's folder closer to the pale blue screen. He left a puddle of spilled folders on the floor behind him.

"Laith!" I groaned, kneeling to put them back in some kind or order, but everyone's pages were mixed together. "How are we going to explain this?"

Laith let out a string of curses, slamming Victoria's folder onto the desk.

Abandoning my impossible task, I jumped up and leaned over his shoulder, just as he dropped his head onto the desk and let out a hoarse cry. I tugged the papers out from under him and left him to his histrionics—*What was it Victoria said about shifting giving him a sense of control?*

My eyes roved the messy comments page until I picked out some of Mardone's handiwork. *Lazy. Insolent. Reactive.* Holding the folder so close to my face, I got a sudden whiff of fresh ink. Little marks all over the page began to glow.

Holy shift.

Not only had Mardone written those terrible things herself, but she'd been systematically editing other professor's glowing reviews to fall more in line with her own, like changing *appealing demeanor* to *appalling demeanor*.

"Why would she lie like this?" I let the folder fall, unsure if Laith had any way of picking up on Mardone's edits, or if he only knew about the comments she'd written.

"To get her out of the way." Laith shook his head miserably and muttered, "Dammit, Victoria, I knew this was a stupid..."

A thunderous roar rattled the floorboards. For a moment, I thought it was one of the bears, but then I heard a door opening and closing, and the thunder took on a metallic quality.

"Someone's on the stairs!" I hissed.

Laith straightened up and recoiled at the sight of the mess he'd made. Another string of curses left his lips and he grabbed two handfuls of his hair. "Hurry! Help me!"

Voices gathered outside the third floor door, which luckily Laith had also thought to lock, but already a key was fumbling at the door knob.

"There's no time," I growled, grabbing his shoulder and spinning him to face me. "Kiss me."

"What?" he yelped as the outer door swung open.

"Kiss me." I grabbed him by his tuxedo lapels, pulling his face close to mine. "And kill two birds with one stone."

His brow wrinkled for the briefest of seconds, and then his eyes grew wide. He got it.

His hands slid around my waist in the same moment that I jumped backward to sit on Mardone's desk, sweeping my skirt in a wide path that knocked aside everything that wasn't already on the floor. My arms encircled his shoulders, my fingers tangling in the curls just above his cape, and in the flash of breath before his lips touched mine, I realized I had seen this all before, that day I caught his scent in the cafeteria after he'd tried to warn me...

Laith Brighton kissed me, his lips as soft as his stubble was rough, and the rush of fiery prickles I had braced for never came. Even so, I made an embarrassing noise of relief, which, thank goodness, he must have mistaken for part of the ruse because he let out an equally mortifying groan. A key clicked into the office door, and Laith leaned in, bending me backward.

Victoria! You're doing this to save Victoria!

The door swung open and the light directly over our head blazed on, nearly blinding me even through my tightly shut eyelids.

***

In the middle of the night, the window behind the pacing Chancellor had become a dull mirror, reflecting the faintly distorted images of everyone gathered in the Board Room—the Gladwells, all three Deans, the golden wolf sitting smug in his usual chair, Laith in handcuffs, and me.

The Chancellor rubbed the back of his head. "Well, this is certainly some kind of pickle we're in. I've got Lenore telling me Dan is a Manip, and Dan telling me Laith is the Manip—"

"It's not Laith!" I slammed my fist on the table and pointed at Helms. Rough red lesions encircled his neck where Belhollow had shaved him down to pink skin—to assess how much damage I'd caused, I guessed. "But that fact that you're letting that monster sit there like some kind of fancy house pet tells me you've already made up your minds."

"I'm sorry, Remi," the Chancellor said. "I realize that either way, this night has been very hard on you, but Dan's version makes a lot more sense. Manips are much more common among mountain lions—"

"I have been helping Laith train his mind for two and a half years now," Mardone said. "If he were a Manip, I would know about it."

"Not if he doesn't want you to," Helms voice oozed into my mind, and I flew out of my chair.

"You stay out of my head!" I shouted. "I know what you did."

"Remi, please sit down," the Chancellor said. "You are perfectly safe—"

"Let her talk, Oberon," the Vice-Chancellor snapped from her chair near the head of the table. "Hers is the version I'm most interested in."

"Yes," Belhollow echoed, coming over to stand beside me. "She's the one all this happened to."

The Chancellor sighed and dropped into his chair. "Very well. But if she's under the influence of the mountain lion, I don't see how—"

"His name is *Laith*," I snarled. "And he's the only reason I'm not... I don't even *know* what Helms was going to do, and frankly I don't really *want* to. But I do know that on the first day of class, I started shifting in the bookstore and..."

For the second time that night, I told about the reverse shift, and his private confession, and the creepy time loss during the dance, and the attempted kiss, and the hand where it wasn't invited, and the anger when I tried to leave. And, once again, I left out the part where I could smell the disgusting truth all over him.

"I can't explain it," I said, when they asked how I knew it was him, as though everything else about his behavior wasn't incriminating enough for me to have made an educated guess. "It's like my wolf was barking, telling me I had to get away from him. And then it all just clicked."

The golden wolf yawned. *"And moments later, that* litter-sitter *over there conveniently showed up with some contrived story about a dance emergency."*

"That part is true," Mardone said with a triumphant laugh. "Miss St. James' pack mates were causing quite a disturbance. I sent Laith to look for her myself. Which is why I then went looking for him when he never came back."

The golden wolf fidgeted in his chair. *"Ah, well, all the same. He had the opportunity, and as we saw in your office, no small amount of motive."*

"Believe me, *Professor*, no one is more disappointed than I am with these two's complete lack of respect for my personal property. However, I don't see how that has any bearing on your claim. From where I stood, their feelings seemed extremely mutual." She curled her lip with disgust. "Perhaps it was *you* who flew into a jealous rage?"

"*I shifted to protect my student,*" Helms shot back. "*And look what it's gotten me. Trapped! Same as Remi! I couldn't do that to myself.*"

"He makes a good point," the Chancellor said. "And besides, all this talk about him making a pass at Remi... that's obviously someone else putting ideas in her head. Everyone knows Dan doesn't swing that way."

The golden wolf yelped.

The Vice-Chancellor buried her face in her hands. "Oberon, *please.*"

Dean Embry rolled back from the table with his hands up. "I'm not touching that."

Dean Mardone threw her head back and laughed. "Are you insane?"

Dean Belhollow swore under her breath and turned to me, whispering, "Honey, I am so sorry."

The Chancellor's brows furrowed as he took in all of our reactions. "We *do* all know that, right? I mean, I never would have let a female student take private lessons with an instructor if..."

Another chorus of groans filled the office.

"Stop speaking, dear," the Vice-Chancellor sighed. "Just... stop... speaking."

The golden wolf placed both front paws on the table. *"Ah, yes, well, actually, that is true. I've been quite open about it. I'm surprised you don't remember me showing you, um, my, er, partner's photograph. It's in my wallet, if you'll just let me run back to my apartment..."*

Laith banged both handcuffed fists on the table. "He's doing it right now!"

The Gladwells and all three Deans blinked their eyes and shook their heads, like they'd all had one of those split second dreams where you're falling off a cliff.

"You see?" Mardone shrieked. "It's him!"

The golden wolf sat back on his haunches, eyes rolling wildly. *"No! That was* him! *He* made me say that!"

The Chancellor launched to his feet, nearly knocking his chair over. He stalked back and forth, ferociously rubbing the sides of his head. "How the hell are we ever supposed to figure this out?"

"I don't know, Oberon," Belhollow snapped. "Perhaps we could listen to Remi?"

It occurred to me that the Chancellor's behavior was so unhinged because someone in this room had the power to bend everyone else to his will, and that meant the Chancellor was currently not the most powerful shifter on his own campus.

But he never really has been, has he?

"Ms. Shirley!" I shouted.

Now it was my turn for everyone to look at me like I was insane. Even Laith.

But not the golden wolf. He cocked his head to one side and narrowed his eyes. He was the only one who knew what kind of risk I was taking—if I was even taking a risk at all. But given the disturbing letter from the Tooth and Claw Society, I feared that may have been the one thing about which he was honest.

"Ms. Shirley," I repeated, glaring right into Helm's eyes. "Call her in."

The Chancellor scratched his head. "I'm not sure what a librarian is going to bring to the table, Remi..."

"But she's not *just* a librarian, is she?" I turned my gaze on the Gladwells. "She can smell things."

The Vice-Chancellor tilted her head. "We can all smell things, Remi. I've got to agree with my husband on this *one* thing." She shot him a hard look.

I took a deep breath in through my nose and out through my mouth. Just like the Chancellor taught me. "Ms. Shirley has the scent-sight. Or did you seriously believe no student has ever noticed she can literally read our schedules with her nose? It's not just some parlor trick."

The Gladwells exchanged glances. Mardone and Embry shifted uncomfortably in their chairs.

"Doesn't miss a thing, does she?" Belhollow patted my arm. "And she's right, of course. We should have thought of it ourselves."

The golden wolf turned an anxious circle in his chair. *"This is absurd! Dragging the poor old woman out of bed at this hour!"*

The Gladwells held each other's eyes for a long moment before the Vice-Chancellor nodded.

"You can't be serious!"

The Chancellor narrowed his eyes at Helms, his first shrewd look of the night. "It's the fastest way to clear your name, Dan. I would think you'd be relieved."

The golden wolf stamped his paws and glared down the length of the table at me. It seemed my gamble might pay off. If Helms outed me, he would never get the chance to take me back to Hawtrey. The Gladwells would hold on to me forever.

The Chancellor sank back into his chair, took a deep breath, and closed his eyes. Five seconds later, they popped open and he smiled. "She's on her way."

Several minutes passed.

And then several more.

The Chancellor drummed his fingers on the table.

"Oh, for Heaven's sake! Gareth, go carry her up here!"

Dean Embry left, and then returned a few moments later with Ms. Shirley—still wearing her fluffy white Academy-issued robe—cradled in his arms. Before he had even set her tiny feet on the floor, she began coughing.

She waved her hands in front of her face. "What died in here?"

The Vice-Chancellor stood and walked around the table, laying a hand on the old woman's shoulder. "Ms. Shirley, would you mind telling us what you see when you take a good whiff of Professor Helms over here?"

Ms. Shirley's moon eyes stared vacantly around the room as the Vice-Chancellor guided her over to Helms' chair. The golden wolf kept turning in circles and whining.

"Stay still, Dan," the Chancellor commanded. "If you're innocent, you have nothing to fear."

Helms sank to his haunches, his whole body leaning away as Ms. Shirley pushed her wiggling nose toward him. She took a long, deep breath...

And vomited all over his paws.

Everyone groaned and gagged.

Ms. Shirley scrambled backwards, wrinkled hands clasped over her mouth. "Get this creature *out* of here!" she moaned through her fingers.

Snarling, the golden wolf leapt right over her head...

And crashed head first into Belhollow's shaggy black bear chest.

Whoa, how did she shift that fast?!

She sank her yellow teeth into Helms' furry shoulder and flung him back onto the table. He slid down the length of it, leaving a skid of blood all the way down to the suddenly-appeared white and black wolves' waiting jaws.

The golden wolf came up on his three good legs and lunged for the black wolf's throat. With a window-rattling roar, Dean Embry's grizzly bear charged into the fray, with Belhollow right behind him.

Laith—whose chair had rolled back from the table with the force of Helms' landing—lurched forward, even in his handcuffs, but Dean Mardone caught him by the back of his shirt and yanked him and me both from the Board Room. She slammed the doors behind us.

"You should have let me shift!" Laith shook out of her grip, nearly topping over in his unbalanced state.

She gave him a withering look. "In handcuffs? You'd have cut your paws off.

A nauseous shudder rolled through my body as a wolf shrieked behind the door.

Are they killing him?

Is he killing one of them?

"Ms. Shirley!" I suddenly realized. "They'll trample—"

"Right here," she chirped from just below my line of vision.

Laith dropped down on one knee in front of her, the handcuffs still clasping his hands together so that he looked like he was going to propose. "Ms. Shirley, I think you just saved my life. How can I ever repay you?"

She yawned. "If you could just carry me back down the stairs so I don't break my neck, we'll call it even."

Laith looked from his handcuffs to Dean Mardone. She hurried into the Vice-Chancellor's office and came out with a tiny key. She took Laith's hands in one of her own, caressing his fingers as her other hand turned the lock. The cuffs popped open and Laith cast them aside, rubbing his reddened wrists.

"Is it safe for us down there?" Laith asked.

"Just don't *dawdle*," she said, glaring at him and then even harder at me. "The Gladwells sang all the angry little puppies a lullaby and they went back to their rooms."

"What about the bears?" I asked.

She rolled her eyes. "They do whatever the dogs do. Now go. I need to get back in there. We'll talk about how you defaced my office tomorrow."

Laith caught my eye. Was he blushing? We would need to talk about *that*, too.

We did it for Victoria, I reminded myself.

"Ready, Ms. Shirley?" Laith asked.

"As I'll ever be," she said with a mischievous grin.

Laith scooped her up in his arms. As her face rose level with Dean Mardone's, she wrinkled up her nose. "You don't smell so fresh yourself, Lenore."

CHAPTER EIGHTEEN

"I can't believe finding out Ms. Shirley sleeps in a dog bed under the book store stairs is *not* the most disturbing thing we discovered tonight," I said with a shudder as Laith and I pushed through the double doors into the empty Great Hall.

Laith let out an exhausted-sounding chuckle. "Hey, sleeping shifted is totally a thing. You'll have to try it now."

A blush crept up my cheeks, and I was grateful that even after all the chaos, someone had remembered to dim the chandelier to its normal nighttime setting. Sleeping shifted sounded a lot like sleeping naked, and sleeping naked sounded a lot like something you might wind up doing with someone after a hardcore make-out session on a professor's desk.

"I mean, now that this is all over. Not *right now*," Laith clarified so quickly that I had to wonder if his words had given him the same mental images.

Don't, Remi. He only kissed you to cover his tracks and hopefully get Victoria out of Dean Mardone's cross hairs. And that's the only reason you kissed him.

My shoulders sagged. "I don't think anything is over."

"No," he said slowly. "But at least you can shift again."

I shook my head. "If I could shift, I would have shifted when..." I stopped. I was going to say *when we kissed*, but he definitely did not need to know that. "When Helms attacked."

Laith smirked, a wildly inappropriate reaction to that statement, which made me think he knew exactly what I really meant. After all, he had admitted to feeling something strange when we touched.

But it could just as easily have been revulsion!

"And anyway," I said, gesturing upward in the general direction of the Board Room. "For all we know, he's up there getting inside all their heads. I mean, how do you even contain someone like that? Is there anything he couldn't talk his way out of?"

"For all we know, he's dead." Laith shrugged. "But even if they didn't tear him into the tiny pieces he deserves, his power is gone. For you, anyway."

"I don't think you understand," I said, my voice cracking. "He did something to my head. *For months.* He... I can't just snap my fingers and be over it."

"Hey, whoa. I'm not saying that at all," Laith said gently. "I can't even imagine what this must have been like for you, or what recovery looks like, but I..." He raked his fingers through his hair. "You remember the fail-safe mechanism? Manips can override it, yeah, but only as long as you don't know what's happening. Now that you do..."

"The spell is broken," I murmured, and I was certain that all across the state of Alabama, Hickoree and half a dozen long-lost foster sisters were smiling in their sleep.

Laith took a deep breath and closed his eyes. "We're only as powerful as our ability to keep our secret."

I took several steps backward, and even with his eyes closed, he winced.

"What do you mean we?" I whispered. "You're not... you can't..."

He opened his eyes, and it felt like he'd fallen off a cliff into a pool of his own self-loathing. "It's not something I'm proud of, but I am." He lowered his head. "I understand if that means you need to keep your distance, but I'm telling you so you'll know. I could never hurt you now." He glanced up. "Not that I ever *would*."

My mind reeled. My pulse thundered in my ears.
What kind of terrible taste in men do I have?

"Does Victoria know?" I asked, suddenly thinking of all the times he'd made their relationship sound like some kind of business arrangement, not an affair of the heart.

"Of course she knows." He looked offended for a second, but shook it off. "Mardone, too. But no one else. And I... I need it to stay that way."

I didn't have to ask why. The wolves had been so anxious—almost excited—to blame it on him. If they found out now, or even a year from now, they might rethink everything that happened tonight. It might not matter what Ms. Shirley said. I drew in a sharp breath.

"I need to smell you."

Laith's eyebrows jumped. "Beg your pardon?"

"Just come here." I beckoned him closer with both hands.

He obeyed, his brow furrowing under his messy swoop of hair.

I laid my hands on either side of his chest, felt his lungs moving his solid muscles up and down, his heart pounding just beneath his ribs. And I breathed him in.

To be perfectly honest, he did smell pretty rank. Like an entire football team's worth of sweat had been dumped over his head to celebrate his courtroom victory. There was the iron tang of blood, too, and I knew his tattered tuxedo was hiding more than a few wounds. There was also something like the sour smell a cat sometimes makes when you startle it, which I didn't want to think about too much.

But there was nothing to be afraid of.

Except perhaps the images flicking in the back of my mind that were of a decidedly romantic nature. My heart sped up. The last time that happened, the images came true.

No, Remi!

I pushed away from him and made a big show out of sneezing. "Sorry, it's just all that dander..."

But he didn't fire back. His eyes were the size of saucers. *Milk saucers?* I giggled at my own stupid joke and probably looked crazy. The late hour was finally catching up to me.

"You're like Ms. Shirley," he whispered. "Well, you know, except hot."

"Don't," I said, ignoring the fluttering, flapping storm of butterflies his words had caused in my stomach. "Ms. Shirley could have been a total babe."

"A thousand years ago."

I slugged him on the shoulder, and he grinned. The way I wished he wouldn't.

"You can't tell anyone," I said quickly. "It's... maybe not so good for me."

He crossed an X over his heart.

I crossed one over mine for his secret too.

He started to smile, but it faded before it got very far. He cocked his head and squinted at the air over my head. "You hear that?"

I mimicked his posture. There was a faint sound filtering through the building's thick walls, a sort of choppy buzzing like when the groundskeepers mowed the sprawling lawns, but the grass had turned yellow weeks ago. Also, it was the dead of night.

There was a commotion beyond the front door. Incoherent voices muffled by the heavy wood. The buzzing noise grew to a dull roar. Laith's eyes widened and he darted for the nearest window overlooking the front lawn. I lifted my skirt and ran after him, pressing my face against the glass just as an enormous beam of light swept across the circular driveway. Dust billowed out of the yellow grass and plumes of mist rose from the fountain.

My first sleep-deprived thought was: *Oh, no! Now aliens are real too!*

Laith swore. "That can't be good."

The window rattled against our noses as the shiny black helicopter dropped straight down from the sky onto the lawn. Two pairs of black-clad figures leaped out and raced toward the entrance. One pair carried a stretcher, the other a steel cage.

"Definitely not good," I agreed.

A few moments later, we heard the distant echo of feet clattering up the faculty stairwell, and then, in what seemed an impossibly fast eye blink, they came clattering back down. The black-clad figures hurried back toward the chopper, slower now with the weight of their loads—a golden wolf in the cage, a black wolf on the stretcher.

Laith swore again. "That's the Chancellor."

My fingers curled like claws against the window. The Chancellor had been a serious ass during that whole ordeal, but who knew how much of that had been Helms trying to steer things where he wanted them? Either way, I didn't like seeing him limp under that white sheet.

At least it's not pulled over his head.

The Vice-Chancellor followed in human form. After both wolves were loaded, one of the dark figures helped her into the chopper, and almost immediately, it lifted off the lawn and disappeared into the black sky.

Laith and I turned away, both of us leaning against the window. One of the front doors creaked open, and the three Deans crept inside. Belhollow and Embry wore robes, since turning into a bear can really do a number on your evening wear. Mardone's bright red gown bore dark brown splotches of blood.

"Dean Mardone." Laith trotted toward her, and she met him halfway, throwing her arms around him. I bristled.

For Victoria's sake, obviously.

Laith pushed her away, far more gently than she deserved, but I realized now that keeping his secret safe with her might not be free. He gaped down at her dress. "Are you alright?"

She waved a hand through the air like it was nothing. "It's the Chancellor's, not mine."

"Is he okay?" I asked, coming up behind Laith.

Mardone immediately glared at me. "He's probably lost an eye."

Guilt coursed through my veins. If only I hadn't accepted that dance. If only I hadn't kept quiet about how Helms 'helped' me on the first day. If only I hadn't let Ms. Shirley's warning freak me out to the point that I started shifting. If only I hadn't been so stubborn all those nights in the woods when the wolves called to me and I refused to listen. I could have been here at the beginning of the summer, I could have...

"This is all my fault," I groaned.

Belhollow marched briskly over to us and took my face firmly in her hands. "None of that, baby girl. You're the hero of this story. Do you hear me?" She gently shook my head. "A Manip that powerful... he would have been in charge by the end of the year. But your clever thinking..." She gathered me into the human version of a bear hug. "You saved the whole Academy tonight, honey."

Mardone sniffed. "That seems a little dramatic—"

"Nobody asked you, Lenore," Belhollow snapped, letting me go. "And unhand that boy!" She pointed to where Mardone had linked her arm through Laith's elbow. "I swear on the moon, as long as I'm in charge, we're going to have much stricter guidelines on appropriate student-teacher behavior."

Mardone untangled herself from Laith, who I could tell was biting the insides of his cheeks not to smile. "I'm going to bed," she huffed and began walking away. "And so should all of you." She tossed her hair over her shoulder and gave me one last death stare. "Your *own* beds."

Looks like Operation Save Victoria may have been an immediate success.

As soon as the door to the faculty apartments slammed shut, Belhollow shook her head. "I'm sorry, Laith. I see how she is. If it were up to me, she would have been on that chopper out of here too."

Laith shrugged. "Thank you, ma'am. But I can handle her."

Belhollow tsked. "Even so. That's not something a student should ever have to do." She turned back to me and smoothed my hair. "You come to my office tomorrow, Remi. We'll get you any help you need to recover from this."

Dean Embry shuffled forward, bowing his head. "I owe you an apology, St. James. You can consider your mid-term grades erased."

"Thank you, sir," I said, because I refused to utter the phrase 'It's okay' to anyone who had made me feel as badly as he'd made me feel about myself for the last eight weeks.

He nodded, and without another word headed toward the faculty door.

"Is the Chancellor going to be okay?" I asked, when it was just me and Laith and Belhollow.

She offered a tight smile. "He should make a full recovery, with or without the eye."

I shuddered at the thought of Helms' fangs sinking into the Chancellor's face.

Belhollow patted my shoulder. "Get some rest. Tomorrow, we'll start fresh."

And then she was gone, too.

Laith and I looked at each other, and somehow I knew that he wasn't any more ready to be alone in his room than I was. So we ambled onto the dance floor, keeping a good two feet of space between us. My gown trailed limply alongside my bare feet; I didn't have the energy to hold it up anymore.

And who even knows what became of my shoes...

Laith stuffed his hands into his pants pockets, his shoulders hunching under his black cape. "So..."

I laughed nervously. "So..."

We weaved around each other in unsteady circles, as though we were just two normal kids walking back to our normal dorm rooms, completely exhausted and maybe the tiniest bit buzzed after a perfectly normal Halloween party.

"What do we tell Victoria?" he asked.

My heart cracked—not broke, that would be way too dramatic for Remi St. James—but I knew what I had to say. "We tell her the truth before Mardone does it for us. We tell her we didn't know how else to explain the mess we'd made, so..." I swallowed hard, steeling my voice to sound like it meant this. "So we kissed, and it was super weird and we... we didn't like it at all."

His forehead crinkled. "We didn't?"

Ugh, there's the arrogant Laith Brighton I know and hate. Of course his ego expects a gold star for a fake kiss shared under extreme duress.

I shot him a disgusted glare.

Even though, technically, he *did* deserve a gold star in the department.

But he never needed to know that. I hardened my glare.

"I mean, right." He shook his head and set his jaw. "We didn't. It was exactly as sloppy as I would have ever expected from kissing a dog."

"Really?" I shot back. "Because for me, the problem was that your tongue felt exactly like your stubble."

He scowled. "Yeah, well, at least my breath doesn't smell like a little rubber *Wall Street Journal*, Miss... Dandy Dinmont."

I laughed, the embarrassing kind that sounds more like an obnoxiously loud hiccup. "That's not even a real dog."

"It's a terrier. Look it up."

"You know," I said, turning in a delirious circle around him, "I've never met another cat who knew so much about dog breeds."

"Keep your friends close." His hand caught mine and lifted it over my head, turning my lazy circle into a twirl that ended with us inches apart. He flashed a sleepy, devious grin. "And your enemies closer."

"If you strangle a man together, can you really call yourselves enemies?"

He cocked his head, a little smile playing on his lips. "Friends then?"

I wrinkled my nose. "Um, no. I was thinking more like allies. In the war against... whatever it is that's happening here."

He nodded slowly. "A crime-fighting duo. I like it."

"Exactly." I smiled and tweaked his lapel. "You're a born sidekick."

His eyes darted to my hand. I started to pull it back, and then hesitated. I knew I shouldn't ask what I was about to ask—he was practically engaged—but I also thought Victoria would understand why I needed to. I had to record over the sensory memories of Daniel Helms' hands.

I chewed on my lip. "It's pretty messed up that the only people we danced with tonight were our pervy teachers."

He chuckled, soft and low. "Yeah." And now he bit his lip. "You want to fix that?"

I nodded, my throat suddenly tight as my hand came to rest on his shoulder. He rested one hand lightly on my waist and lifted our other hands into the air, and our feet began to move in a halting waltz to the silence of the Great Hall.

"Thank you," I whispered, hoping he understood that this wasn't me putting the moves on him.

He shrugged. "What's one waltz between a hero and her sidekick?"

"Ow! Watch it!" I yanked my bare toes out from under his shoe. "I thought cats were supposed to be graceful?"

He shook his head, biting the corner of his lip. "Nah, that was all you. Typical canine. Always getting underfoot."

My forehead fell forward, and I let out another embarrassing laugh, that kind where you make a farting sound with your lips and accidentally get spittle on your date's lapel, but you're both too tired to really care.

Um, Remi? He's not your date, remember?

I lifted my head and inched back, putting a more appropriate amount of space between our hips.

The mischievous smile faded from his mouth, and he cleared his throat. "I was actually asking what we should tell Victoria about the dean's list."

I turned my face away from his, taking in the creepy, abandoned remains of the Halloween masquerade—the buffet tables lined with stale desserts and cold hors d'oeuvres, the spiderweb-style streamers hanging from the balconies, the giant bats soaring on either side of the chandelier. Half of this I hadn't even noticed before. All I'd been able to think about was whether Professor Helms was going to notice me.

I shivered all the way down to my core.

"The truth about that, too," I said firmly. "If someone's out to hurt her, then she has to know."

Laith nodded. His hand gave mine a little squeeze.

And that was when it hit me.

No prickles.

My eyes darted from our clasped fingers to my hand clutching his shoulder to his hand gently holding my waist. And I guess I must have forgotten not to gasp out loud.

"Whatever it was," Laith said slowly, "I think it ended when we kissed."

There was no use denying it then. He had felt the prickles too.

Or something.

I forced a nonchalant laugh. "We must have scared it away."

He gave me a rueful smile. "Should make life a lot easier, huh?"

I stared down at his shoes, which had finally stopped landing on my toes. "How long—?"

"Since the first time we shook hands."

I snorted. "Is *that* why you're such a grouch?"

"Don't flatter yourself, Poodle. My piss-poor attitude pre-dates you by at least eighteen years." He laughed, but it turned into a loud yawn.

His hand fell from my waist, and he twirled me one more time before taking a long step backwards, still holding onto my hand. He squeezed it once, and then his fingers loosened. I let it drop back to my side.

"I don't know about you, St. James, but I could sleep for the next twenty-four hours."

My eyelids sagged, but I couldn't resist one more shot. "Isn't that about average for someone like you?"

Laith groaned and spun away from me on his heel. "Enough with the cat jabs! You're on your own now." He stalked a few paces away and then swung back around, his eyes heavy but concerned. "You okay with being alone now?" He came closer, pointing at the couches along the wall. "Because if you're not, we can sit right there 'til the sun comes up."

His words made my heart flutter, but the thought of the couches made my skin crawl with memories of Helms. I wanted the night to end as far away from anything that reminded me of that monster as possible.

Laith's brow creased. "Now what?"

I followed his gaze. A small pair of headlights was bouncing up the driveway. They came around the loop and disappeared in front of the building.

"Who could that be?"

"Oh. Duh," he said, smacking himself on the forehead.

He jogged back over to the entrance, just as the double doors swung open again. Victoria came in, carrying a rumpled overnight bag, followed by the pale, lanky, bespectacled bear-guy that Xander and Kanze had dubbed Creepy Crayon—aka none other than Jake Powell. He carried a bag like Victoria's in one hand, and dragged an enormous rolling suitcase behind him with the other.

A third figure appeared, this one short and round, her arms laden with cardboard boxes that hid her entire head, except for a shock of electric blue hair. She tottered through the door and Jake shut it behind her.

Victoria's face lit up when she saw me and Laith—mostly Laith, obviously.

"Hey, babe," she said through a yawn. "You waited up for me."

They kissed each other on the edges of their mouths and shared a quick hug.

"How was the Halloween party?"

Laith glanced at me and laughed uneasily. "Oh, it was a night to remember."

Victoria squinted at him. "Sounds like I need to hear about it. Just let me get the new girl settled..." She leaned in and whispered, "Late bloomer."

The new girl wiggled her fingers in greeting around the edge of a box.

"I can help her," I blurted, excited for the chance to be as unlike Winter Davenport as humanly possible. "You and Laith go ahead and catch up."

"Perfect." Victoria beamed at me. "She's going to be in 2J. It should be unlocked."

I walked over to Jake and the new girl, reaching for the rolling suitcase. Jake pushed it toward me, and as soon as my fingers closed around the handle, he was stumbling toward the guy's stairwell.

"Goodnight, Jake!" Victoria called. "Thank you for your help."

He waved a hand over his shoulder and disappeared.

"That dude is so weird," Victoria muttered. She looped her arm through Laith's. "Now, tell me about this night to remember before I forget to stay awake."

I turned toward the new girl, tugging her—*wow, incredibly heavy*—suitcase. "Hi, I'm Remi, do you need me to carry—"

The cardboard boxes slammed to the floor with an echoing *thud*. The blue-haired girl standing over them clasped both hands over her lower face, stifling the high-pitched shriek emanating from her mouth. The suitcase handle slipped out of my hand and another loud thud filled the room.

No. Freaking. Way.

CHAPTER NINETEEN

I woke up to soft yet insistent knocking on my door.

Rolling away from the sound, I came face to face with two dozen bars of bright light blasting through my blinds. I tugged my pillow over my head, solving both problems at once. Or so I'd hoped. But the knocking only grew louder.

So help me, if that's Hickoree...

Growling, I tossed my pillow aside and threw the covers off. I snuggled into my fluffy white robe, which was kind of like wearing my bed wrapped around me like a burrito, and so took some of the sting out of waking up. I quickly lashed the belt around my waist and checked the lapels to make sure everything was tucked in properly. No need to start the day with a private peep show for whoever had dared to disturb my slumber.

My money remained on it being Hickoree, that improbable come-from-behind winner of last night's bizarre Halloween plot twist contest. She had still been talking a mile a minute when I finally had to excuse myself—and by excuse myself, I mean I shouted *"Goodnight, can't wait to hear more tomorrow!"* and literally ran out the door. But I stayed long enough to learn that Hickoree had hated Keller Parks because her creative writing professor would only let her write about her *truth* and not magic, and she had given him quite a surprise. Victoria and Jake had to do a little memory re-adjusting on that poor guy—all shifters are basically Manips when it comes to non-shifters.

Which makes us all creepy as hell actually.

But I didn't tell that to Hickoree. I didn't tell her any of the many unflattering things I'd learned about Gladwell Academy last night. Hickoree was going to be the most enthusiastic student in their thirty-year history, so I didn't see much immediate danger for her of making the dean's list.

Whatever that even means.

But when I opened the door a crack to tell her to please let me go back to sleep, it wasn't Hickoree's overeager face waiting for me. It was Victoria, two steaming to-go cups of coffee, and one paper sack that I didn't need the scent-sight to know was full of bacon, egg, and cheese croissants.

Victoria smiled way too big. "I come bearing gifts!"

I swung the door open all the way and Victoria slipped past me, setting her gifts on my tiny dining table. As soon as the door clicked shut, she threw her arms around my neck.

"Remi, I am *so* sorry! Laith told me everything. I just can't believe it." She pushed me out to arms-length, but still clung to my shoulders. Then her eyes widened in horror. "I mean, I *do* believe it! Of course I believe it! I just meant—"

"Victoria, relax," I said, taking her by the shoulders too. "I get it. I can't really believe it either."

She let go of me abruptly and turned toward the table. "Do you want to sit down?"

I chuckled. "I think that's supposed to be my line, but sure."

We dropped into the seats and Victoria unpacked the croissants while I took a life-giving gulp of hot coffee. Sitting at the table felt weird. I normally just flopped down on the couch to shovel food into my mouth if I wasn't just eating in the cafeteria with the nerds.

Oh, crap. There's another weird thing from last night I'll have to deal with today.

Victoria handed me one of the croissants wrapped in crinkly butcher's paper, and I sank my teeth into the melty, crunchy, flaky goodness. "Mmmph. This is everything I needed. You are an angel, Victoria."

"I don't know about that." Victoria's eyes tightened and she looked down at her own croissant. Instead of stuffing it in her mouth like a normal person—meaning me—she tore off a tiny piece to nibble on.

I swallowed my bite and took another swig of coffee to steel my nerves. "So... Laith told you everything?"

She sighed and nodded. "Yeah. I'm kind of reeling. I don't know what to think anymore."

I cringed. "I understand, but listen, you have to believe me, it didn't mean anything. I didn't know how else to cover up the mess he'd made, and so I just said it, and he did it, and, honestly, it was awful, I swear. I'm glad I'll never have to do it again!"

Victoria tilted her head and squinted at me with... amusement? Was that right?

"Remi, I'm talking about finding out that my name is on a list of students to be turned over to some sort of secret society. Are you talking about the kiss?"

Heat flamed over my face. I stuffed the rest of the croissant into my big mouth so I'd be stuck chewing for the next thirty years until Victoria and Laith were happily married and living in some big fancy house in Dallas or something.

Come to think of it, where do *shifters live?*

Victoria laughed. "Have you been worrying about this all night?"

I nodded, my cheeks bulging like a guilty chipmunk.

"Remi..." Victoria sighed. "Okay. I guess we can do this part first."

I kept chewing.

Victoria took another dainty bite and a sip of coffee. Then she just stared at her croissant for a long time, making several false starts at speaking.

I kept chewing. *Wow. I might die eating this thing.*

Victoria took a deep breath through her nostrils and placed both palms on the table as she slowly exhaled through her mouth. "I haven't been honest with you, Remi. I didn't think of it that way because I've been lying to everyone every day for so long, but when you asked me in the woods if Laith and I were serious, and I let you think we were, like, getting married someday or something..." She winced and shook her head. "That was too far. And I see now that it may have been really unfair to you. And to Laith."

I swallowed with an audible gulp, leaving my mouth too dry to speak. But whatever was coming next, she apparently needed me to ask, because she had grown quiet, staring once again into the seemingly infinite mystery that was her breakfast, or lunch, or whatever this was. *What time is it anyway?*

"I don't understand?" I finally croaked, reaching for my coffee.

Victoria stood up and paced my tiny kitchenette, stepping over my lifeless ball gown again and again until I finally stuck my foot out and snagged it out of her way. She locked her fingers behind her head and did the breathing exercise again.

"Victoria?"

"Laith isn't my boyfriend," she blurted, but at my fridge instead of me. "I don't have a boyfriend. I don't *want* a boyfriend. And I should never have asked Laith to help me keep that a secret. Or I should have let him stop when..."

When what?!

My heart beat wildly against my ribs. My skin prickled—shift prickled, and for the first time in two months, I felt that dizzy, blood-rushing thing obscuring all the logical thoughts in my brain. I gripped the edges of the table and slammed on the brakes.

This is not about you, *Remi.*

"Victoria..." I stood up and touched her closest arm, which was now folded tightly across her chest. She was shaking.

"I understand if you hate me," she said quietly. "I see now that I may have been causing you unnecessary pain."

"What?" I squeaked. "No. I don't know what you mean."

She gave me some serious side-eye shade. "You haven't acquired a taste?"

"No! No way! Laith? Me? Never! He's such a jerk!" I backed away, shaking my head.

"Okay." She shrugged. "If you say so. But he... well, never mind."

He what?!

Victoria turned toward me. "I'm sorry, Remi. Even if I've totally misread the way you blush every time he walks by. You still shouldn't have had to spend any time last night worrying what I was going to think about some crazy hot kiss you two shared on top of Dean Mardone's desk."

"Crazy hot?" I yelped. "I didn't say anything about it being crazy hot."

"No." She lifted her eyebrows. "*You* didn't."

I slumped back into my chair, mind reeling. Apparently, that mortifying moan of his was *real*. I didn't even know what to think about that. The last twenty-four hours had been... a lot.

Without a thought, I reached over and grabbed Victoria's croissant and began chomping ravenously away.

Victoria laughed and nudged my shoulder. "Now you're stealing my breakfast, too?"

I dropped the croissant in horror. "Why am I such a terrible person?"

"It's fine. You deserve all the croissants, Remi."

Spoken like the truest of friends.

Victoria sat back down. "And anything else you might be craving either." She lifted her hands defensively. "Just saying!"

I guzzled down the last of my coffee and set the empty cup down. It fell over.

"You want my coffee, too?" Victoria pushed it toward me.

"No!"

That was a lie. I totally did.

Victoria leaned across the table and touched my hand. Then she yanked it away, as if her revelation had put some sort of glass wall between us. I reached over and grabbed her hand.

"Hey. You don't have to be afraid. I'm not going to assume you want to join my reverse harem or anything." I narrowed my eyes playfully. "Unless you do?"

She squealed and buried her face in her hands. "No! I mean, no offense. But I..." She bit her lip shyly. "You remember when I said I missed the food in Texas?"

I raised my eyebrows. "Uh-huh?"

She blushed. "I miss the person who *makes* the food."

I grinned. "And I'm guessing that's not your mom?"

She shook her head. I could see she was biting back a grin.

"That's really great, Victoria. I'm so happy for you."

And for me...

I mean, what? No. Cut that out. Laith Brighton is still... a long way from being boyfriend material. A very long way. Remember the poor elk?! And then there's the whole thing where he can manipulate brains, just like the guy who manipulated your brain. Even if he can't, even if he wouldn't do that... it's still in him. That's a lot to process.

"But I'm going to need you to see through what you started," Victoria said, cutting off my rambling inner monologue, suddenly all business-like.

I cocked my head. "What do you mean?"

She lifted one eyebrow. "You kissed Laith to explain away his mess *and* draw Mardone's attention away from me, right?"

"Right," I said slowly.

"Well, then, it's time for us to switch places. Or else what was the point?"

"I don't think I'm following..."

She sighed. "Listen, I am not the least bit afraid of Lenore Mardone. She's the lowest-ranking Dean, only got promoted from Professor two years ago. As a mountain lion, her opinions hardly even matter to the others. They're just required by the Board to have a fully representational staff."

"Wait, I thought they *were* the Board. The Gladwells and the three Deans."

"Definitely not." Victoria laughed, and even though she didn't mean it cruelly, it made me feel very young and naive.

How should I know how school administrations work?

"Who do you think owns the Gladwell Academy?" Victoria asked.

"Um... the Gladwells?"

"Nope. The Board. The Gladwells *used* to own it, but they had to sell out. So now there's a Board, and they decide how things are done here. And they decided that the Gladwells had to have a diverse staff. Before the Board, everything was very lycan-centric."

I stiffened. "Oof. They don't put that in the promo video, do they?"

"No, but it is all on the record. I did a research paper on the history of the school last year. You can fact check me with Ms. Shirley. The Gladwells aren't really ashamed of their past species-ism. If you ask them, they'll just say their views have 'evolved.' I know because I asked them. Anyway, where was I going with all this?" She scrunched her forehead.

"Dean Mardone. Her creepy dean's list."

"Right." Victoria nodded. "If she's made some sort of shady deal to ship graduates she doesn't like off to this... what was it?"

"Tooth and Claw Society," I said.

"Yeah, them. Whoever they are. Whatever they want with us. It's probably safe to assume Mardone is working alone, but—"

"So shouldn't we just tell the Gladwells. Or, I guess, Belhollow right now?"

Victoria pursed her lips. "I don't think so. Not yet. We need to know for sure who all is in on it. What if every Dean has their own list?"

I shook my head. "Embry, maybe. But Belhollow? No way."

"We have to be certain," Victoria said firmly. "If we go to the wrong person, we might just all end up on a list."

I leaned back in my chair. "So what do we do? Just ignore it and hope nothing happens?"

"Oh, hell no," Victoria said. "We're going to get to the bottom of this. I am *not* about getting trafficked to some seedy shifter underbelly or whatever this is. Or letting anyone else be either. Which brings me back to what I started out to say. As an intern, I'm in a much better position to do some investigating than you are, or even Laith. So, if you want to help, the best thing you can do is take being Laith's fake girlfriend off my hands and keep Mardone distracted."

My jaw dropped. "You want me to pretend to date Laith?"

"Don't worry, it's super easy. If I can do it, anyone can." She smiled brightly. "He's super low maintenance, except be careful with the hair." She whispered, "He spends *hours* on it."

Really? It looks so effortless...

"What? Victoria, no! I can*not* pretend to date Laith. Why does that need to be part of it?"

Victoria sighed like this should be very obvious. "Because Mardone is holding Laith's secret over his head. Someone has to be a buffer to keep her from... *increasing* her expectations of him. Plus, if all she's thinking about is how to get rid of you, she's more likely to make more amateur mistakes like leaving her incriminating paperwork lying on her desk in plain sight." Victoria rolled her eyes.

I squirmed in my chair. This did not seem like a fool-proof plan. This seemed like a plan that ended with me being made a fool of.

"I don't know." I chewed on my lip. "What does Laith think of all this?"

CHAPTER TWENTY

Laith dropped his tray next to mine on the table. "Hey, babe."

The nerds' mouths dropped open, revealing way more of their pizza than I needed to see. They had done a sufficient enough job of groveling for forgiveness when I came downstairs for dinner that I decided not to expend any extra effort on torturing them with the suspense of whether or not I would grant it.

Who among us hasn't danced with the enemy?

I elbowed Laith in the ribs when he leaned in for a cheek peck. If I was going to pretend to date the hottest guy on campus, he was going to have to step up his game. It may have worked for Victoria, but I was ready to be treated like we already spent our Friday nights playing gin rummy.

"Rule number one: If you ever call me *babe* again, I will neuter you."

His golden flecks sparkled. "You prefer yappy dog breeds?"

"Yes, actually." I leaned in to his ear and whispered, "It will remind me that I don't actually like you."

He scowled. "You got it, Puggle."

I drew in a sharp breath and reminded myself not to hit him. "Okay, just, *no*."

"Um... what's going on?" Xander asked, pushing his glasses up on his nose like he needed to see us better to believe it.

"What does it look like?" Laith drawled, sliding his arm around my chair. "Remi and I had... a really nice time at the masquerade."

Oh, great, make me look easy. This is why I'm only pretending to date him.

Kanze narrowed his eyes. "I thought Remi was almost kidnapped by a Manip who'd been keeping her from shifting and you strangled him together and then he woke up and ate the Chancellor's eye?"

There had been a special assembly this morning before I woke up in which the rest of the student body had been filled in on our Halloween escapade.

Parts of it.

Laith grinned and shrugged. "What can I say? We really enjoy a good strangling."

I let my forehead hit the table top. *Why does everything he says sound so wrong?*

"Hi, Remi! Can I sit here?" Hickoree chirped from just behind me, and wow, just like that, I was happy to have her here.

I lifted my head and found Xander staring wide-eyed at a point just behind my shoulder. I turned and came to face to face with that same screen print of those damn actors from that damn TV show.

Seriously? Wearing a shirt about a supernatural TV show to your first day of supernatural college? Isn't that a little like wearing a band's T-shirt to their concert?

Lifting my eyes to her face, I started to give Hickoree a hard time, but my mouth clamped shut when I saw the googly-eyed expression she was making. I followed her gaze back to Xander... and realized for the first time that the random list of names on the T-shirt he was wearing over a long-sleeve shirt were from that same terrible TV show.

He scrambled to his feet and stuck out his hand over the table. "Hi! I'm Xander! I love your shirt!"

Hickoree held his hand for way too long. "I'm Hickoree. Like the tree. But with two e's. Like a tree."

"Wow," Xander breathed. "That is so cool."

Kanze glanced up and rolled his eyes.

Same, buddy. Same.

Hickoree sat down and immediately launched into a run-down of her top ten favorite episodes, which quickly turned into twenty, but who's counting?

Me. I was. Because I kept thinking surely it was about to be over, but by episode number twelve, it was obvious now that Hickoree was here, this was *never* going to be over. Eventually, Kanze sighed, grabbed his tray, and stomped off.

"Yikes," Laith said quietly. "Trouble on Geek Street."

"Rule number two: Only *I* get to make fun of my nerds."

Laith grinned. "You sure do have a lot of rules."

"You think two is a lot? We've barely even scratched the surface. Which reminds me, rule number three is no sharpening your claws on the drapes."

He waggled his eyebrows. "Is that an invitation to see your drapes?"

"No. It is not." I made a little *hmph* sound. "We haven't even had our first fake date."

"What? Last night definitely counts."

"Um, no."

He propped his elbow on the table and leaned his head on his hand. "Okay, but come on, tell me the truth. Now that you know I was never really a smarmy philanderer—"

"Feline-derer," I whispered, about to crack myself up.

His eyebrows flattened. "You're a laugh riot, St. James."

"I'm sorry. Go on, you were saying?"

He cleared his throat. "I was asking if maybe you wanted to change your opinion on my kissing skills. Now that you have the full picture?"

I ducked my head, pretending to be really interested in the last pizza crust on my plate. "Nope. All decisions are final."

He groaned and let his arm flop onto the table. "You're killing me, Poodle."

A shadow fell over my plate. "Hello, James."

Ugh, not now!

I turned in my chair, finally ready to chew Winter Davenport the new one she deserved, but I stopped short. She had her arms clasped behind her back in what appeared to be a close approximation to a posture of humility.

"Hello, Port."

She ignored the new nickname I had come up with on the spot, and took a deep breath. "I just wanted to say that what happened to you was really messed up, and I hope you get your wolf back so I can be better than you fair and square."

My mouth fell open. "Um, thank you?"

She nodded curtly, flipped her hair, and hurried back to the table with the rest of her pack.

"Well, that was... special?" Laith offered.

I pushed back from the table, grabbing my tray. "I've got to go."

Laith started to stand up. "Are you o—"

"Sit. Stay." I rolled my eyes. "I know those words probably aren't in your vocabulary."

But Laith did settle back into his seat. *Good boy.*

"There's just something I have to do," I said. "Alone."

***

The forest rattled with dry leaves as a cold wind whipped through the trees. Goosebumps rose all over my naked body as I tucked my clothing back into the tunnel entrance so nothing would blow away. And then I crawled carefully over the slick moss to the tip of the rocky outcropping where I had sat with Victoria two weeks ago, before that first private meeting with Helms.

I shuddered, and not from the cold.

A full moon hung just over the mountain across from me, and even though Helms had drilled it into our class that the lunar cycle had nothing to do with shifting, I couldn't help but feel like it was going to help.

I crouched on my heels, fingers gripping the edge of the rock. I focused on my breath, lifting and sinking in my chest, the air from my lungs becoming one with the wind that swayed the trees. I tried to do the thing I always refused to do during Mardone's class, which was to watch my human thoughts float by on the river of consciousness until they became fewer and fewer.

I could hear Dean Embry barking at me to just do it. Just shift. But I didn't understand how to make the wolf come out when it wasn't the wolf's idea.

Just ask.

I licked my lips. Things couldn't get any more ridiculous.

"Um, Wolf Remi? Me? Hello, I don't really know how this works. But if you, uh, if you want to come back now, you can."

Not even the slightest prickling. Aside from the multiplying goosebumps.

"It's safe," I said, my voice growing stronger. "He's gone. He's not coming back."

Did I really believe that?

And if not him, wouldn't there maybe just be someone else?

"Okay, I guess I really don't know how safe it is here. Things are pretty weird. But I do know..." I swallowed a sudden lump in my throat. "I know that I wouldn't have gotten away without your warning. You saved me."

A whine started in the back of my head and then moved into my throat and out my lips.

I saved me.

My heart sped up, blood rushing into my brain and all my limbs with pounding force. The forest tilted, and I looked down in time to see my fingers shortening even as my nails lengthened into claws. I gasped, those claws scratching the rock as every muscle spasmed and my brain exploded into a million tiny points of light.

I sat back on my haunches, tail sweeping across the moss, and lifted my muzzle to the stars that were singing just for me. I howled, a terrible, beautiful, eerie sound that echoed across the wilderness like it was bouncing right off the moon.

And then, somewhere way behind me, from the other side of the stone wall, another voice joined in. And another, and another, and another, until it seemed even the wind had stopped to listen.

My powerful leg muscles bunched and I sprang off the rock into the forest, my massive paws carrying me over a carpet of pine needles and dead leaves, over fallen logs and trickling streams, until I was standing on the other side of the campus, on the knoll looking down on the buildings with their warm yellow windows and the wolves still singing their impromptu song.

This was my home.

And I was going to fight for it.

CHAPTER TWENTY-ONE

Brown leaves frolicked across the yellow grass, driven by a strong breeze that would have been chilly had I not been wrapped head to tail in my own glorious fur coat. Tomorrow, we would all be shipped home for the holidays—from Thanksgiving until New Year's—so today, we were allowed to spend as much time shifted as we could manage. Get it out of our system.

A black wolf and a white wolf—Xander and Hickoree—scampered after the leaves, snapping them in their jaws and watching the tiny piece float away. I couldn't tell if they both thought this was genuinely great fun, or if they were both pretending for the other.

My nose showed me a gray wolf creeping up the other side of the little hill we'd staked out for our pack. *And three... two... one...*

Kanze rocketed into plain sight, barreling his shoulder into Xander's side and sending the black wolf rolling through the leaves. He came up snapping and the two boys reared up on their hind legs, scrabbling at each other's faces and chests with their big hairy paws. Hickoree yelped and scooted out of their way as they went tumbling tail over tail down the hill.

She walked up and sat beside me, wrapping her fluffy white tail over her paws. The funny thing was that she still had an electric blue streak down the top of her head.

"It's not fair," she whined. *"I like them both. Xander is so sweet, but Kanze... I always did have a thing for swimmers."*

I thumped my tail against the ground and wolf-laughed. *"Dream big, Hickoree. Have them both."*

Somewhere down the hill one of the boys squealed in pain.

"Yeah, I don't think that's going to work." She huffed, sinking down with her head on her paws.

"Well," I said, getting up on all fours. *"I'm going to leave you three to sort it out. The Gladwells want to see me now that they're back."*

"Good luck with that."

I trotted down the hill, past the boys, who were chewing on each other's ears, and back to the sidewalk that led up to the courtyard behind Therian Hall. I was walking under one of the small trees that still had most of its leaves when a yellowish-brown snake dropped down right in front of my face.

I yelped and scooted backward.

Laith's laughter drifted into my head.

Not a snake then. A fuzzy tail. I snapped at it, and he flicked it just out of reach.

"Nice try, Poodle."

I looked up and there he was, muscular feline body slung over the lowest branch.

He peered down at me with half-lidded amber eyes. *"All ready for our Texas adventure?"*

Laith and I couldn't talk to Victoria very often around campus with the whole charade we had going, so we were secretly meeting up with her in Texas to talk about what, if anything, she'd been able to learn so far. Before Gladwell, I had never even left the state of Alabama, so I was pretty excited for the change of scenery, even if it was going to be a month full of awkward moments. The last two years Laith had gone home with her, he was pretending to be her boyfriend for her family's sake, too. But not this year.

"*I'm socially exhausted just thinking about it,*" I said.

Laith sighed. "*You're such a waste of a perfectly good feline, you know it?*"

"*You wish,*" I barked.

His ears twitched, which was about as much of a mirthful expression as his serious mountain lion face could muster. I had to admit, my wolf-self did not find his cat-self at all attractive, because.... nature, I guess. But his human-self got harder for my human-self to resist every day, because also... nature, I guess.

"*Got a meeting with the Gladwells,*" I said. "*See you at dinner?*"

"*Okay, but here's an idea. What if, just this once, we didn't sit with the people I'm not allowed to call nerds, but who totally are nerds, I'm sorry?*"

"*Laith Brighton, are you finally asking me on a proper fake first date?*"

He sniffed his pinkish-red nose. "*No, I'm asking for a little peace and quiet before the socially exhausting situations commence.*"

"*We'll see,*" I said, trying not to wag my tail as I walked away.

I went back to my room and shifted—it finally made sense why there were so many scratch marks in the hardwood floor—and threw on some clothes, which honestly felt weird after several hours spent with my 'clothes' growing out of my skin. They just sit there on top of us, all loose and fluttery and... weird.

I grabbed a stack of books I needed to return to Ms. Shirley—books that had seemed like they might have some mention of Tooth and Claw, but no such luck—and headed for the tower. I dropped the books off on the counter, careful not to disturb Ms. Shirley, who was asleep in her dog bed under the stairs. She hadn't been feeling well lately, which was sad, and also kind of scary. Helms' warning still rang in my ears.

The faculty door in the attic was propped open with a flower pot full of dead mums. I hurried up the spiral stairs. Being in the stairwell by the door always gave me gross memories.

"Remi!" The Vice-Chancellor rose when I walked into her office and came around the desk to hug me. "It's so good to see you again. How are you? I hear you've become something of a shift whiz since we last met."

I shrugged, but couldn't hide my grin. "It's definitely not a problem anymore."

"That's wonderful. Here, have a seat." She touched the back of a chair. "The Chancellor will be here in a moment."

I sat down. "Is he doing okay?"

"Oh, you know men. Always such babies. But he's fine. Don't let him fool you."

As if on cue, The Chancellor limped into the room. His cheeks were a little sunken and he wore a black patch over his left eye. "Remi," he said, and his voice sounded thin, almost frail.

He came over to my chair and dropped down on one knee with a grunt. His one eye darted between both of mine. "I owe you a tremendous apology, Remi. While I would like to blame my behavior entirely on that *Manip*," he sputtered, "I'm afraid I was also just a foolish old man. Can you forgive me?"

Victoria's words about the Gladwells having to be forced into species diversity rang inside my head. "Thank you, but I'm not the one you really need to be asking. Laith could have been killed that night. He deserved better than that."

The Chancellor winced. "Yes, of course. We will be speaking to Laith soon." He stood with another grunt. "I'm just happy we had such a clever student here to come up with that idea to call Ms. Shirley."

The Chancellor sat in the chair next to me. The Vice-Chancellor had already taken up her perch behind her desk. She folded her hands now and peered at me. "Tell us, Remi, when did you realize that Ms. Shirley possessed the scent-sight? And don't say it was because she can sniff out the books. That's a trick most shifters can master in no time. But the scent-sight..." She leaned forward. "That's something *much* different."

I squirmed in my chair. "I didn't know it had a name. I just knew that she could read with her nose. And the rest was just a lucky guess."

The Chancellor bent over, his elbows on his knees. "That's a pretty big jump from reading a book to reading people's souls."

I shrugged. "Like I said. Lucky guess."

The Vice Chancellor tapped a pencil against her temple. "Are you sure you've never experienced anything like that yourself? Maybe without even realizing it?"

I chewed on my lip like I was thinking about it, and then shook my head. "No, ma'am."

"Because we've been wondering..." The Chancellor clasped his hands together. "We've been wondering if maybe that was how you realized what Helms was yourself?"

"No. I already told you. He wasn't acting right. And then it just dawned on me." I shrugged again. "That's really all."

The Gladwells exchanged an unreadable glance. The Chancellor leaned back in his chair and crossed one ankle over his knee. "Okay, if you say so."

"But if you ever do experience anything like that," the Vice-Chancellor said, "it would be very important for you to let us know immediately."

Had Helms squealed at some point? Had he realized he was never going back to Hawtrey and made a plea deal? What if they had accepted it? What if he was still out there?

My heart sped up, and I felt my wolf pushing against the edges of my skin, but I silently told her to stay. It worked remarkably well, I had discovered these past three weeks.

"It's an extremely rare gift," the Chancellor said. "And extremely valuable, as you've seen for yourself.

It's also how we are able to locate new shifters. So anyone who possessed that gift... well, they would be very well taken care of."

I couldn't hold back my incredulous stare. "Ms. Shirley lives in a dog bed under the stairs."

Both Gladwells laughed—kind of nervously, in my opinion. "Ms. Shirley is a character, alright," the Chancellor said, fidgeting with his eye patch. "We've offered her much better accommodations, time and time again."

"So please don't let that deter you, if you have anything you'd like to say," the Vice-Chancellor said, eyes urging me to spill it.

And maybe I should. I mean, Ms. Shirley really was old and who knew how many of her screws had come loose. And Helms... well, why should I believe anything Helms ever said? My gift, as they called it, had been a little overwhelming since I'd started shifting again. My days were full of uninvited whiffs and their corresponding images. It was distracting, and I feared it was only going to get worse.

What if that's what made Ms. Shirley blind?

I licked my lips, and maybe I was going to confess and maybe I wasn't. I'll never know, because at exactly that moment, I caught one of those whiffs. It took every ounce of strength in me not to turn my head in the direction it was drifting from, but I knew any movement like that would give me away.

I drew in a regular breath, holding it briefly inside my lungs so my brain had a chance to work out what it was trying to show me. I smelled manila folders and paper and ink. I couldn't be sure, but I thought it was coming from the filing cabinet off to the side of me.

The Gladwells watched me closely. I swallowed the lump of fear rising in my throat. Something about the smell was triggering my lupine alarm system.

"I don't have the scent-sight," I said. "I promise."

The smell jammed itself up inside my nose, making it suddenly hard to breathe. A series of images flashed through my mind, indecipherable, except...

Rahm?

I latched onto his face, pulling that image in for closer inspection.

And that's exactly what it was. An image. A photograph. Clipped to a stack of papers tucked into a manila envelope. Just like Jake's. Just like Victoria's.

Did they find him?

Excitement built in my chest with every breath. If they had a picture that recent—one I'd never seen on his social media—then they must know where he is. Were they going to tell me that next?

Play it cool, Remi. Be patient.

But then words came into focus. His name. His age. His...

His species?!

I must have let out a surprised whimper because both Gladwells leaned forward with concern—or interest—brimming in their eyes. I heard them distantly asking if I was okay, but I waved the questions off, trying to focus on these words that made no sense.

My brother wasn't a shifter. That was impossible. The Gladwells had told me so.

But there it was. Clear as if I were looking at a page resting on the table.

Rahm St. James, age 18, early admission, gray wolf.

My fingers gripped the edge of my chair as the words started to float away.

No! Wait!

There was something more flickering at the edges. If I could just get a better smell... I pretended to sneeze. Well, half-sneeze. The kind where you suck in the air and then nothing comes back out. I made a show out of rubbing my nose.

The scent swirled through the maze of my brain and punched me right in the heart as the next line of words became clear.

Alias: Robert Borden

Status: Culled

***

End of Book One

Second Semester Starts Now:

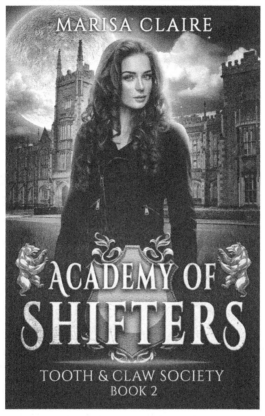

VIP List: Sign up to be the first to get the latest news about the Academy of Shifters series.

More Books from Marisa Claire:

Dragon Games: Legion Academy

Thank you for reading Academy of Shifters: Werewolves 101. If you enjoyed reading this book, please remember to leave a review on Amazon. Positive reviews are the best way to thank an author for writing a book you loved. When a book has a lot of reviews, Amazon will show that book to more potential readers. The review doesn't have to be long—one or two sentences are just fine! We read all our reviews and appreciate each one of them!

www.tormentpublishing.com

Acknowledgements:
Special thanks to Torment Publishing! Without you this book would not have happened. I love you guys.
Thanks to all the early readers and the support of my fans.
Thanks to my family for their support!

Credits:
Chase Night – Editor
Jack Llartin – Editor

Made in the USA
Monee, IL
13 January 2021